I0586490

A SHOT OF TREASON

A MARY MACCALLAN NOVEL

Paula J Longhurst

Ingram Spark in Association with Open Flame Press

Open Flame Press

Publisher's Note: This is a work of fiction. Names, characters, places, and incidents are a product of the author's imagination. Locales and public names are sometimes used for atmospheric purposes. Any resemblance to actual people, living or dead, or to businesses, companies, events, institutions, or locales is completely coincidental.

Book Layout © 2018 BookDesignTemplates.com

A Shot of Treason/ Paula J Longhurst. -- 1st ed.
ISBN 978-0-9989258-1-3

To Joyce Chacksfield.
Thanks Mum, for always letting my imagination soar!

Acknowledgements

One sunny Friday afternoon, not long after Case of Espionage was published, a customer, we'll call her Nancy, came in, pounded her perfectly formed fist on the desk and demanded a sequel. I hadn't planned to do a sequel but I'm a firm believer of striking whilst the iron is hot. My thanks go once again to Anne H, Linda G and Ann C for beta reading. To Bob, editor extraordinaire, Chris, for cover design, moral support and the purchase of a 3D model of the Palace of Westminster and of course to the amazing customers and staff at King's English Bookstore in Salt Lake City.

CHAPTER 1

LOCH-MACCALLAN'S
INTERNAL PRESS RELEASE
PRIVATE AND CONFIDENTIAL

Garrett Maccallan is now on bereavement leave; He has appointed Mary Maccallan acting CEO until his return. Feel free to contact me with any concerns.

Phillipa Forrester, Head of HR. LM 2006

Summer 2006

It took me three tries to find Seb. Starting at the first pub just off Vauxhall bridge and working ma way out from there. He and the barman are the only people in here. The place is the bad side of dingy if the greasy surface of the bar is anything to go by; hidden horrors of housekeeping lie in the shadows. The barman looks me up and down, takes in the suit and the heels, which are hurting like hell at this point.

"He yours?"

I really should have taken my time before answering that question, but I'm so pleased I found him, I claim him straight away.

"Are you a spy too?" The cloth in the barman's hands moves rhythmically over the glass he's holding; the Guinness logo will be polished into oblivion any minute. I decide to use my native Scots accent, with bells on.

"Nae, man, I'ahhm, jist 'is minder."

"Well get Walter out of here, he's making my place look untidy. If I had a pound for every bloke who claims to be a spook around here, I'd be rolling in it. Oh, and he's running a tab."

His name is Seb not Walter. In his drunken state did he use an alias? The poor bastard just had his career flushed down the khasi, so it's nae surprise that he cracked and turned to drink.

Even though he's had to give up his dry cleaning habit; this morning he was whistling as he ironed a shirt, even after he burned his fingers doing so. That same shirt is now crumpled, whiskey staining the sleeve that I can see. As I move closer the three empty glasses obscured by his elbow come into view. I pull out my wallet.

"Three scotches?"

The barman's grin widens, "Doubles."

I groan and hand him a fifty.

Careful to stand back a bit I place the tips of my fingers on Seb's shoulder, "Hey, hen. C'mon now."

The alcohol may have blunted his reflexes but he still opens his eyes, looking up at me, his pupils huge.

"S'Mary," he levers himself upright almost knocking the empty glasses flying, "Shee, there's Mary."

"C'mon Walter," I say, not wanting to blow his flimsy cover, "Let's get ye home."

"Who S'Walter?" he blinks, befuddled. He tries to get off the barstool and ends up in a heap at my feet. Grinning like an idiot he uses me as a climbing frame to get vertical. The barman doesn't bother to conceal his amusement. Once Seb's upright, swaying a little, the barman adds a parting shot.

"You and your tart, sling your hook."

Seb grinds to a halt, he turns.

"Don you call my girl a tart, she's a respeck, respeck, re-specky lady, bossy." He draws himself up to his full height. "She runs," he stops, groping for the company name, "MacDonalds."

"And I," the barman says with contempt, "Am the bloody queen of Sheba. Get out!"

The cab I came here in is still circling. I flag him down but he can't really stop anywhere so he slows down enough that I can open the rear door, shove Seb in headfirst, and pile in after him.

"Where to, Missus?"

"Victoria," I say, buckling Seb in, and then myself. Seb rests his head on my shoulder and falls sound asleep. When I turned the cab around and dropped off Jo, my PA, so that she could catch another cab to see my father off to his Swiss clinic eyrie, I knew I was making a choice. I chose to go and rescue a washed-up spy from himself.

Late October 2006.

I've been top banana at Maccallan's for three scant months now. The annual Women in Business Initiative luncheon just broke up where, due to a little maneuvering by Jo, I ended up sat next to Chalmers, the T&I secretary. I charmed him with my swotted up knowledge of old bangers, which I know he collects.

Chalmers and I are amongst the last to walk out onto the street.

"Didn't know you were such a car buff, Mary. Your father is of course. Perhaps it's genetic," Chalmers muses. "Remind me to invite you both to the Goodwood Festival of Speed next year."

I make a mental note to find out the date of the festival and be out of the country.

"Can I drop you somewhere, Mary?" Chalmers signals his car; a large black limousine rolls toward us.

I'm about to accept when I notice a familiar figure crossing the road, waving at me.

"Nae thanks, I promised this chap an interview."

"Oh, I've met him," Chalmers looks where I'm pointing. "One of the new boys at the Independent. Very personable chappie. I say, what's wrong with his arm?"

"I'll ask him," I say. "Don't let me keep you."

I wait until Chalmers releases me from a thankfully chaste hug. After watching the secretary climb into the back of his waiting car, I turn to Daz Patel, interning junior business correspondent for the Independent. Also the least devout Hindu and most accident prone human being I've ever met.

"What the hell happened to you this time, hen?"

Daz got his journalism degree from the University of Bangalore. He told me he wants to see what working at a real newspaper is like before they go extinct. He is direct and for a journalist still surprisingly idealistic. As always he wears a cream raincoat, but this afternoon only one arm is through a sleeve; the other he holds in front of him as if cinched in an invisible sling. Tiny dots of dried crimson spot the bandage wrapped around his forearm like ink spread on blotting paper.

"I almost got mugged last night."

He lets me release the safety pin holding the material in place, I unwrap it and—

"Almost!!"

I'm glad that we were the last to leave. There's no one else to overhear my outburst. His arm looks like a jagged map of the pyramids; more dried blood, shiny in this light.

"Sakes man, you should see a doctor. That looks mingin'!"

"Go to an NHS hospital?" Daz holds his good hand up in horror, "home of germs and flesh eating superbugs, I'd rather die first."

"That's a knife wound. You're lucky it didn't sever an artery!"

"How come you know so much about knife wounds?"

"I'm Scots, hen. We'd call this," I gesture at the wound, "Saturday night."

"Do you want to know what happened or not?" Daz clumsily rewraps the arm and I re-pin the bandage.

"Of course I do, but not out here."

I flag down a taxi and coax Daz inside.

"Where to?" The cabbie enquires.

"Victoria, please." I look at Daz. "If I see any fresh seepage spots I'm taking you straight to hospital."

Monday afternoon traffic is the usual capital mess. We crawl along. Daz keeps up a flow of chat, I think mainly to prove to me that he's not about to collapse in a pool of blood.

Just before the coach station at Victoria we slow to molasses speed.

"Blasted builders," the cabbie says, "they're doing something at the building site over the back there t'day. Gawd knows that expansion's caused enough grief."

The 'expansion' is an add-on to Victoria Place. Recently London's skyline boasts more cranes than the docks at Canary wharf. Skyscrapers are popping up faster than a bad case of teenage acne. Every day it seems there's a road closure as a procession of cement mixers queues up to pour their guts into yet another floor of rebar. The fact I even know what rebar is shows how easily these terms sink into a Londoner's psyche.

"You can drop us here," I say.

"Oh you diamond," says the cabbie, "at least I won't get caught up in that mess for hours."

CHAPTER 2

Daz and I stroll along the pavement until we reach the Loch Maccallan building. The entrance to my flat is around the side but I take him in the front door and into the lift. I get several nods and a "Good afternoon, Mary," from a board member who hates my guts.

I return the greeting and then close the lift doors before he can worm his way in with us.

At the door to my flat, I pull out my keys.

"Seb!" I call out.

There's no answer, must've gone out.

"C'mon hen," I say to Daz, pointing him at the sofa in the centre of the room. "Sit yerself down and take off your coat. I'll get Jo up here; she's a better judge of injuries than me. She'll know if there's anything we should do."

Daz wanders towards the framed newspaper headlines I keep on the wall in ma upstairs office. Headlines like 'The Future's Female' and 'Maccallan Progeny Shatters glass ceiling.' Aye, I know it seems vain to keep reminders of a job I actually still have, but there are some days I feel like I'm swabbing the decks instead of steering the ship.

"Aha," he says, unconsciously checking his reflection in the frame glass, "these are the reason we met."

"Nae Daz, we met because that Alsatian snacked on you in the park as you were jogging past me," I say, watching him wince and shake his head, "Now sit down, before you fall down."

"I was only there because I'd read these," he nods to the collection on the wall, "I was new to the newspaper, I wanted to make a name for myself and what better way than an in-depth interview with you, the Scots Scotch Heiress, turned CEO."

I fold my arms and fix him with ma stone face glare, "I hope the stitches, and the course of rabies shots were worth it."

"The dog? Oh goodness me, no! Being bitten on the bum by the dog was nowhere in my plans. I was fortunate that he bit mostly into the can of pepper spray I had in my back pocket."

My annoyance at being duped by Daz is laced with admiration for the way he handled our first encounter. My guard was well and truly down, because I'd just watched 400 lbs. of hungry predator burst from the bushes and clamp its jaws around unsuspecting prey.

This kind of thing should only be viewed from the safety of a sofa on a Saturday night during a BBC One nature documentary featuring one of the BBC's 'nature Davids', Attenborough or Tennant, (being Scots you can guess which one I prefer) Having it happen in a London park rocked me to ma core. And from a more pragmatic angle if Daz hadn't been there…

After the dog got the equivalent of a vindaloo to the nose instead of a side of succulent buttock and blundered back into the bushes, I 999'd then, melted back into the rapidly forming crowd of Nike, Adidas and Sweaty Betty wearing joggers.

Daz, so pale he could've been mistaken for one of our IT department, and doped up with pain killers, only said one thing before the medics carted him off to hospital.

"Tigers," his voice spacey and muffled by the oxygen mask now sitting over his nose and mouth. "I didn't know they had tigers in this country."

The incident was the 'dead donkey' on the local news that night. They gave it some Hound of the Baskervilles spin. Even had the brass neck to say witnesses called the animal 'exotic looking'. The onlookers just glommed onto Daz's saying 'tiger', and there was only one actual witness, me. The report was a pretty half-assed job. The one thing they did get right, the dog was caught.

After I jelly-legged it back to my flat and asked Jo to come upstairs so that I wouldn't have to tell the same story twice, both Jo and Seb elected themselves nursemaids which did not go down well with yours truly. Jo backed off when I told her to 'stop fussin' woman!'.

Seb still wanted to 'do something' so he joined the searchers combing the park. In the end the dog was undone by a nice juicy steak liberally laced with ketamine. Last I heard it was still at Battersea Dogs Home being 'retrained'.

Daz reappeared over a month later at the café where I always finish my morning jog with a shot of espresso. When I think back, he was clever, he didn't try and get my attention or flag me down mid-jog. I was glad to see him upright so I went over to his table and re-introduced myself. And he flat out said he was a journalist but he was already past my defenses at that point.

Despite now knowing that he sort of engineered our first meeting; him admitting it now almost makes him seem more trustworthy. In fact the only person I trust more is Seb. I wonder where he's got to?

Summer 2006

The cab parks around the side and Seb flows out onto the pavement. He leans heavily on me as we go up the stairs; the bugger weighs a ton and he's stupid drunk. "I luurrvve you," he keeps saying. "Gissa kiss." This last move almost proves disastrous as he leans into me at the top of the last flight of stairs, nearly overbalancing us both. I lean his back against the wall outside my flat so that I can unlock the door. Before I can get the key into the lock he's slid down the wall into a sitting position, his shirt rucked up.

Only a few hours ago he strode out of here ready to take the world by storm. Now look at the poor sod, a drunken wreck. I have to add to his list of indignities by pulling him across the newish carpet so that I can get the door closed, which causes the poly cotton blend of his shirt to crackle as I charge him up with static electricity.

We have nae spoken of that day since. Seb got a handle on his drinking binges, but it wasn't long after that, his benign nocturnal activities turned a lot darker.

Present day

Seb is here. I can see him on the balcony, pacing back and forth, phone clam-shelled to his ear.

I shove the sliding door open and call, "Hey, hen, I could use some of your field medical expertise."

"Sir, I'll call you back."

He avoids my glare because now I know who he was talking to; Arthur Pond, head of MI6 and the reason for Seb's partial unemployment.

"Seb, this is Daz."

As soon as Seb claps eyes on him I wonder if I haven't made a giant mistake. His eyes go wide with surprise and, something else——guilt?

He doesn't question why Daz is there. He simply leans down and shakes his hand. Sitting down on the sofa next to Daz, he takes hold of his arm and, before either of us can stop him, removes the bandage and examines the gash underneath.

"Does he need stitches?" I ask.

Seb shakes his head.

"It leaked a bit initially. What did you use, superglue?"

Daz nods and my mouth drops open.

"Superglue? You superglued the cut shut?"

Seb jumps in before I can say anything else. "It's an old field medic's trick; glue rather than stitches. You army Daz?"

"My brother, he is a field surgeon. He taught me a thing or two about the treatment of injuries. I have a pocket trauma kit with me at all times."

"Wait a minute. They use superglue on the battlefield?" I splutter.

"They use a modified version. Superglue tends to cause an exothermic reaction. How's the burning, Daz?"

"Worse when I first did it, settled down to a dull throb now."

"Okay, my friend. The only reason I can think of for a hospital visit is if you didn't disinfect the wound properly."

"I did," Daz replies. "Lathered up my arm with soap and hot water like I was going to do open heart surgery. Dried it with paper towels and stuck it shut." Seb re-wraps the wound a lot more expertly than Daz did, securing it with the same safety pin.

"Who attacked you?" Seb asks.

Daz raises both arms in a rough approximation of 'I surrender', wincing and letting his bad arm drop.

"I dunno. I was on the tube yesterday evening, last one of the night so it was crammed. Some Dynamo wannabe was doing close up magic in our carriage. It was equal parts cool and annoying because I was sitting down and people kept standing on my foot. By the time we got to Victoria I was running out of toes that still had feeling in them. I got off with a few other people and by the time we'd gone up the steps we'd spread out. I admit I was not paying attention to what was going on around me; I was trying to compose a headline."

"You're a journalist?" Seb's question is sharp.

To me, "He's a journalist?"

"Can we talk about this later?" I say, doing my impression of a woman who doesn't want to take her partner and shake him by the shoulders. "Daz, you said you were distracted."

"Yeah. The next thing I know I'm almost up the stairs to the exit and someone comes up behind me, puts a knife to my throat and demands my watch." He pulls back his unbloodied shirt sleeve to reveal a beautiful old Tag Heuer. "My father gave me this. It was a gift for getting my degree. No way was I going to give it to some mugger. I was fumbling in my pocket for my wallet but all I could grab was my keys when someone else intervened."

I was watching Daz. Now my gaze switches to Seb, who has taken a sudden interest in the view across the street.

"Another man. He pulled the mugger away from me and the knife slashed across my arm instead of my carotid. When I was free, I turned and saw the would-be mugger was struggling with someone all dressed in black; he even wore one of those SAS style balaclavas. Before I ran I watched him toss the mugger down the stairs I had just come up. I could feel that I was bleeding, so I pelted onto the station concourse and blundered into the men's loo. I scared the elephant poo out of the attendant——when he saw I was bleeding he ran away."

"You report this to the police?" Seb asks. "Did you see the mugger's face?"

"I saw his face. He wasn't wearing a mask. He looked average, foreign."

Seb is shaking his head. "Foreign. Are you sure?"

Even if I didn't have some idea what was going on, that question would strike me as weird——and vaguely offensive. Daz, however, is too wrapped up in remembering his ordeal.

"Euro foreign. There was something about him, but the mind plays tricks. I doubt I'd be able to pick him out of a line-up. Once I was sure I'd stuck myself back together I went in search of the man who had helped me."

Seb's mouth sets into a firm line.

"That was pretty daft Daz. Suppose he hadn't been able to contain the mugger. You would've been walking into a messy situation."

"I couldn't just go home without knowing," Daz says with a degree of stubbornness. "I went down the stairs and no sign of either man. All the way down to the platform, still nothing. So I climbed back up the stairs and went home to bed."

"Do me a favour," Seb says. "If you won't go and see a doctor at least Skype your brother. Have him take a look at it. If he tells you to seek medical attention, do it."

Daz grudgingly agrees.

He gets up, collects his things, and walks towards the door. "See you tomorrow in the park, gelati," he says to me.

Time to have it out with Seb over his nocturnal activities. I've been turning a blind'ish eye up to now, but the incident with Daz just brought things to a head. I feel fully justified in what I'm about to do. When Seb moved in we promised each other there would be 'no secrets' and well let's just say that one of us hasn't been keeping that promise.

"Did he just call you an ice cream?" Seb dives in first. He knows that him communicating with Pond rubs me up the wrong way. Thing is, I'm not narked at him for that. And we are going to have this out, because unlike him, I know where this conversation is going.

"Nae hen, you're thinking of posh Italian ice cream. 'gelati's' like the Gujarat version of 'mate' or 'pal'."

"Well, when I'm head of Station I might investigate the different dialects further."

"You don't speak Gujarati or Hindi? You're MI6!" I tease him and watch him relax, "C'mon man, you're slipping."

A Pond expression, the tiniest hint of smugness passes over Seb's face like a shaft of sunlight as he counts on the fingers of one hand. "I speak plenty of languages: Arabic, Chinese, Spanish, Dutch, French, German, Russian."

"Well if I ever need a translator, I know where to come, hen." I walk over to my desk and start to shuffle the documents I signed this morning into a neat pile.

Seb, however, stays where he is, arms folded. "What was that park stuff about?"

"Remember 'Dog-Man'?"

"The bloke who got bitten on the ars? Wait, that's him?"

I nod, deciding that Seb doesn't need to know about Daz's ulterior motives.

"Daz and I have been jogging in Hyde Park every Tuesday morning."

"I thought you didn't associate with journalists much less consider them friends."

"Daz is a special case, hen. I made a promise to look out for him."

"Not immune to the old boy network after all?" I allow his gentle critique. He knows I can't stand the 'who you know' nepotism that our board engenders.

"I had Daz checked out before I started dealing with him. I even fed him a couple of inaccurate stories which he meticulously researched before running a corrected version of one and ditching the other. I got one of those security firms to vet him, stuffed to the gunnels with ex-military."

"Ravenwood?"

"No, the other one, Charteris." I push on. "They gave Daz the all clear and then I got a visit from one of their men."

"Name?" Seb raps out.

"Mr. Keyes." I want to stay focused on what we should be discussing so I root around on my desk and bring over the business card Fletcher Keyes handed me. It's good card stock; Charteris' business cards are thick, hopefully not like the men they employ. "Turn it over." Seb does and his eyes narrow with suspicion.

Daz Patel lied.

"What did he lie about?"

"Patel, his surname is Patil."

"Like the curry guys?"

"Exactly like the curry guys. Daz is Pradesh, Patil's youngest son."

Seb's eyebrows rise into his hairline and no wonder. Curry is an institution amongst the Brits; more of them eat a curry of an evening than they do fish and chips. Patil had figured out the holy grail of fast food: microwaveable curries in a patented steam pouch, chock full of a secret blend of Indian herbs and spices that gives them that 'fresh from the kitchen' taste. They're found in the supermarket freezer along with bags of frozen peas and oven chips. Now they make everything from dopiaza to a full blown vindaloo, with new flavours coming on stream all the time. Recommended by Delia Smith no less when she did her Indian food week.

"Mr. Keyes was carrying a message from Patil senior. Long story short, he asked me to keep an eye on Daz."

"Indefinitely?"

"Couple of years and Daz is back in Mumbai, safe and sound. Patil already has a wife picked out for him."

"And what do you get out of this? You know India is a dry country."

"I won't bore you with the details, but Patil could get us in with a major U.K. supermarket chain, one the old guard have tried and failed to crack. And all I have to do is tell him if Daz looks like he's going off the rails."

"Ah," Seb nods, sagely, "I see."

He has no idea that like a boomerang we are rapidly circling back to my intended topic.

"I've been giving Daz the inside scoop on Maccallan's. He's my media secret weapon. And you nearly got him killed."

"What?" He already sounds guilty.

"Seb, don't try and act all innocent. I know what you've been up to most nights." I start to pace.

"I've been trying to broach this subject for weeks without coming across as a bunny boiler. We go to sleep together but some nights you get up and leave the flat. Some mornings, like this morning, I get up early enough to find you crashed out on the sofa, still wearing your camouflage makeup." I list some of the other things, "The bruised knuckles, how stiff you are some mornings, like you took a beating, or dished one out. I wonder how the head of MI6 would feel knowing that his finely tuned government sanctioned blunt instrument was spending his nights as some kind of "avenging..." I grope for a word that isn't 'angel', "ninja.

"Seb, Pond is just stringing you along with 'scraps'. You must be able to see that. It's time to move on."

"I'm not done yet."

"Done with what?"

"Pond's helping me."

"No, Pond is *using* you!"

The intercom system on my desk (identical to the one downstairs in my actual office) spurts into life.

"Mary," Jo's hushed voice comes over the speaker, "one of the MAC is sniffing around down here. I told him you were on a conference call but he's not going away."

"I'll be right down."

All kinds of expressions have been crossing Seb's face. I pull on my jacket and go toward the door.

"You're going to walk out, in the middle of..."

"Aye, hen, I am. You're pissed off at me? That's the best time to walk away, before one of us says something we'll both regret."

I'm careful not to slam the door behind me. I do strike my heels on the concrete steps harder than I should.

CHAPTER 3

I turn my attention to our MAC problem, one that I can fix. Jo and I (and a few others) have taken to calling the board members the Mary Anning Collection——MAC for short. Anning was a famous fossil hunter and as the board are old, bony, white and three years away from an en masse retirement, this sums them up perfectly.

Last year, while my father was in hiding and I didn't have control of the board, they stopped bickering just long enough to stage a coup. The MAC planted enough doubt in my da's mind that, although I now occupy the CEO's office, my official duties amount to those of a glorified PR person. Oh I'm still getting things done. It just involves talking one-on-one to each individual department and making a chain of smaller moves that don't have my fingerprints all over them. Still the MAC are trying to make me look bad. They poke around my office every few days. Jo is very good at sending them packing, but once in a while it is better that they witness me hard at work at my desk.

At the foot of the stairs, the right hand corridor goes into Jo's office/reception area and from there into the CEO's. Down the left hand corridor sits my old digs. To the right of my old desk is a giant floor to ceiling rectangular white board. A gentle tug on the metal surround opens the connecting door da had installed between the two rooms. My eye is drawn to the desk. A single orange carnation blazes. I take it and carefully insert the flower into the top bottom hole on my suit. Jo has given up asking me where these flowers come from. A flower in the office is code for 'I probably won't be around today'. I've made sure Seb knows how much these little bursts of colour brighten my day.

The board member, Forsythe, looks up when I poke my head out of the door.

"Good afternoon, Percy. Something I can do for you?"

Percy doesn't get up, which doesn't bother me. He makes some trivial excuse about the board meeting for drinks at his club this evening and would I be able to join them. The whole thing is a charade.

I've been tempted on a few occasions to accept the invitation just to see the look on their faces when I walked in, but I don't fancy dying of boredom. Plus the clubs the MAC frequent still don't allow women members, bunch of dinosaurs. Having allowed myself to be seen, and refused the invite, with Jo as witness to the whole thing, I go back towards the office. Forsyth levers himself up creaking as he does so and I get an idea. The MAC aren't the only ones who can make mischief.

"Jo," I call out, whilst old Forsyth is still in earshot. "Please send Secretary Chalmers an invitation to Charlie's 50th birthday bash. Tell him I enjoyed our chat today and would love an opportunity to get his take on some future innovations Loch-Maccallans has in the pipeline."

Jo doesn't miss a beat. "Some flowers for his wife?"

"Perfect." Forsyth seems to have taken root. I pretend to notice him again. "Was there something else, Percy?"

"You met with Secretary Chalmers?"

"Aye, we had lunch today."

"That wasn't a board sanctioned meeting." Forsyth puffs up faster than a bag of jiffy pop in the microwave.

"Nae, it was the Women in Business Initiative luncheon and I was sitting next to Chalmers. He knows my da and it would've been rude to ignore him wouldn't it?" He says nothing. "Well, wouldn't it?"

"Yes, it would." Words might come easier from a stone.

"Don't let me keep you. I dunno about you but I have a ton of paperwork to shoot through."

Forsyth shuffles away. We give it a good few minutes before Jo bursts out laughing.

"You really shouldn't push his buttons. He'd do anything to unseat you, you know that."

"Aye, hen, but if we kow-towed to the Percy Forsyths of this world nothing would get done. And I may have neglected to mention the small TV spot Chalmers and I did for the beeb's business correspondent."

"You'll give the board members a conniption when they see that." Jo smothers another laugh.

"Once the moggy is out of the bag it is damn near impossible to stuff it back in. Now I'd better shift that paperwork."

Despite trying to take the office 'paperless', the old guard refuses to give it up, which is why I have both a physical and a virtual inbox. I turn my attention to the emails.

My godfather and company lawyer, Charlie, is coming up for his 50th birthday end of November and he forbade me to make a big thing of it. So, I'm making a huge thing of it. I have to do it now because he's on his annual month-long trip to Hong Kong. He'll come back with five new suits and a ton of new clients. The venue has been booked for months and now I'm working on the entertainment side of things. Me being me, I went straight for mentalist, Derren Brown. I've been emailing back and forth with his people, but it doesn't look like the dates will work for him. His people suggested a website of approved magicians I might want to check out. Seb and I have been going on a lot of magic show date nights recently because I want to check out the goods before making any decisions.

It's after five when I finish up for the day. Jo poked her head in to say she was going. I take the completed paperwork and put it in the safe. With the MAC poking around, ya can't be too careful. I upgraded security on my office and had a keypad installed as well as the lock. I set both and climb back up to my flat. What am I going to find?

I unlock the door and catch Seb busy on a phone call. Some of his earlier anger appears to have burned off. He has a laptop open on the coffee table and the contents of a file strewn across the floor. I enter and lean against the door to softly close it.

"How did it end up *there*?" Seb asks. "Honestly, Higgins, laptops loaded with sensitive information seem to be attracted to rubbish tips the same way tornados spawn close to trailer parks."

Higgins' voice rings tinny from the speaker on Seb's phone. "At least this one wasn't left on the 6.15 from Euston. Anyway mate, if you could grab it up for me before Pond finds out we've lost another one, I can put the fear of god into the little herbert that 'misplaced' it, and release him back to the job market."

"I'm on it."

"Thanks mate, I owe you one."

Seb hangs up and sees me.

"As you might have heard I have to go and re-trieve an errant laptop. But before I go I've had some time to think about what you said."

Now that the emotion has drained out of the sit-uation he's pretty matter of fact.

"I apologize for not telling you about, well y'know. I, I found a focal point, something I could channel my energies into. Without it I would've gone crazy. I thought you'd be angry if you found out."

If you can call a focal point beating the living tar out of criminals. I think. It's a start, we can build on that.

"I am angry but not with you, with Pond. I know you think he's helping you but I think my analogy is spot on. He's feeding you scraps to keep you around."

"I am fed up of being treated like a tame attack dog too. So how would you deal with my situation. I'm assuming you had a solution in mind."

"Tell Pond that you want your proper job back. Full reinstatement."

He stands silent for a moment, thinking.

"And if he doesn't go for that?"

"You walk. I can think of a dozen companies who would hire you on the spot for the kind of experience you can bring to their corporate security teams. Hell, I'd hire you myself if the bloody minded board would let me."

"That's comforting at least. Er can I borrow a car?"

"Take the Merc,"

I toss him the keys.

CHAPTER 4

One week later

Annoyingly, Pond hasn't had any scraps for Seb to handle. He was pacing like a caged tiger last night. I half expected to hear him slipping out to work over some unsuspecting miscreants so I offered him my body, several times, and managed to tire the poor bugger out. He was dead to the world when I left for the office this morning.

Today has been full of clandestine meetings. As I said, I've found ways of getting things done away from the NHS prescription specs of Percy Forsyth and the rest of the MAC. I have a new ally; our recently appointed head of HR, Philippa Forrester.

Philly, furious that her proposal for recruiting new management talent had been voted down by the board (because I supported it), cornered one of them in the unisex. I was in a stall down the far end and heard her lambast the old, er, gent. "We've got a couple of years until the lot of you shuffle off to fancy villas in Marbella and Costa del, too friggin' expensive for the likes of me," she ranted. "Two years to recruit and promote new talented board members and all you fossils can see is the amount of noughts on your golden handshakes!"

"I've never been so insulted in my life," said the board member.

To which Philly replied, "What a sad sheltered little life you must lead."

"I'll report you."

Philly dared him to do just that.

"I didn't let on that I'd overheard her, just kept an eye on what she did and I liked what I saw. I asked Seb to find any dirt on her: she has a shoe addiction, is a Hufflepuff and goes to Outlander book conventions. Long story short, we teamed up."

The MAC go to their clubs at midday and stay there until at least two in the afternoon, so Philly and I arranged to meet at half past twelve at the new'ish Euro cafe just down from what was Starbucks.

The Starbucks closed a few months back with hardly any warning and has stayed that way. Rumour has it that the lease isn't up yet and the company is still paying the landlord (the City of Westminster County Council), which stops any competitors from stepping into what is a highly desirable location. COW CC didn't hesitate to grant permission for the building next door to become a deli with coffee shop. The owner, a cheery West African with the least English teeth I've ever seen, is petitioning to rent the old building as well so that he can expand.

I catch Philly checking her watch before she looks up. I swear the woman will be early for her own funeral. Woman? Nae. She's a couple of years younger than me with the figure of an Olympic runner. Cascades of thick dark hair are held back off her face by any number of elasticated headbands, the elastic being at the back, the fronts are embroidered, jeweled, or just smack you in the eye bright. It's a look that I haven't a hope in hell of pulling off.

She's standing next to the chalk board they added a week after this place opened.

WELCOME. PLEASE READ THIS.

NEW HERE? A THOUSAND WELCOMES.

NO UNACCOMPANIED MINORS UNDER 18 PAST THIS POINT.

It goes on to detail the four easy steps: Pick, Personalize, Pay, and of course Pick-up.

"What's good here?" is her no-nonsense greeting, softened by a wry smile.

"They do a wonderful caramel latte. I swing between that and their spicy aromatic Turkish coffee. In that one the caffeine doesn't hit you all at once. I worked on a proposal all night a few months back on just one cup."

Philly follows my lead, picking up a small to my medium paper cup, and writing her name on it with the marker provided, along with the number of her selection.

"What a wonderful idea," she enthuses, handing over payment and her cup, and getting a few coins back in return. "Baristas getting to concentrate on making fab coffee instead of cocking up people's names. That Starbucks at Victoria? They somehow translated 'Philippa' into 'Burlap' last week."

I snort with laughter as I lead her over to the pickup point where my latte and her espresso con panna appear.

"You hungry?" I ask, walking over to the bakery counter.

"Hot apple turnover with clotted cream, please." I pay for the turnover and take my order number up to the second floor. I hear Philly ordering a crock madam.

There is music on in here all the time. The owner has a penchant for soundtracks. Hidden speakers pump out everything from James Bond to Harry Potter, which makes the simple act of drinking coffee feel magical. The volume is usually kept low enough that you can talk over the music without having to shout. There's a window seat, I grab it. Philly sits down opposite me.

"Cripes, how did I miss this place," she raves, pausing to sip her espresso. Her eyes almost cross with pleasure. (I know just how she feels). "It's like finding the Three Broomsticks in central London."

"Aye, minus the butterbeer."

The server brings our food. I bite into the flaky pastry and feel the molten apple sear my tongue. Between bites we continue drawing up plans which would severely ruffle some MAC feathers if they ever worked out what we were up to.

When we part company Philly hands me a thumb drive full of personnel files.

"These are all head of department or board material. I've run the usual checks. You'll want to go deeper, I'm sure."

I take my cache back to the flat, intending to sit up on the terrace da and I occasionally use and peruse these via my laptop. Seb is awake and on the phone when I unlock the front door.

"Yes, I'm authorized to view the footage," he says. His professional voice can come across as downright unemotional. "There is a gentleman outside your office right now. He has a data transfer device and written permissions from my director. You can either load the device or upload the information directly to my secure connection. You choose." He hits mute.

"More scraps?" I ask, keeping it light.

"Not this time. Someone stole a tube train right off Victoria Underground's Platform 2."

"How the hell do you steal a tube train in the middle of London with security cameras everywhere?!"

"Well clearly it's not impossible. But all signs point to an inside job. You don't just hop into one of those things and drive it away."

"When did this happen, hen?"

"A week ago." He can see the consternation on my face and moves to head me off or defend his boss or both. "Pond's got a lot on his plate right now and his crack team are off 'firefighting', which leaves the crap team who couldn't find their backsides if you handed them a map and a torch. So now it's been filtered over to me."

The laptop dings and Seb returns to his call.

"Thank you for your assistance, I'll be in touch." He hangs up and swiftly calls off his colleague. "I'm thinking ex driver with a grudge. They're sending me a list of the most recent set of layoffs. I'll start with them."

"I don't get it." I take a seat next to him and lean into the sofa, resting the back of my neck against the soft nap. His hand comes to rest on my leg. "There's no gain for whoever took it. I mean it's not like London Underground, sorry 'TFL', don't have a shed full of more engines and carriages."

"Something else the C team missed," Seb says. I know he's heard me and that the answer will pop out in its own time. "The train was scheduled for routine maintenance. Their logs show that. But if you go further back the same train got a clean bill of health two months previous."

"Who put in the maintenance order?"

"They used the supervisor's code, but that doesn't mean it was the supervisor. And you're right, there is no gain, no disruption. Unless he needed it for something?" Seb's weight moves from the sofa.

"He? Ahhhhhhhhhhhh." The pads of Seb's fingers, ease a morning's worth of tension from my shoulders. He continues to knead, thinking out loud.

"There's something else. That was the same night your friend Daz was almost mugged. I chased the mugger onto platform two and I was almost on him when he jumped onto the rails and legged it into the tunnel. I ended the chase right there. It would be madness to go charging into an unlit tunnel with electrified rails."

"You, ahhh, saw the missing train, *before* it went missing? Lower, ohhh, just there, perfect."

"No, the train that went tech was the 8:15. Your friend from the colonies was on the last train of the night."

His fingers stop, both palms smooth down from shoulder to upper arm. That means he thinks I'm knot free and he's right. My stress reservoir has reset to empty.

"You were around the station the entire night and didn't see anything. Some pretend superhero you are."

He laughs at the superhero comment.

"Any connection between the mugger and the missing train, hen?"

"Doubt it, although," he sinks into a thought and I leave him to it because I'm gasping for a glass of water to dilute that second cup of coffee.

"Are you allowed to tell me any more? Or is the rest above top secret?"

I was compelled into signing the official secrets act last year, long story, best not gone into here.

"Not much to tell. According to a couple of witness statements the train pulled up to the platform. There was an announcement about a relief driver. Then, as people were getting on, another announcement from the cab that the train was going out of service and to get off. Which the passengers did because we unconsciously do as we're told more than we'd like to realize. Train pulled off and vanished into thin air. It was only when the replacement driver arrived that he realized the train had gone. He had the presence of mind not to blab that to the passengers."

"And they didn't shut down the station?" The clink of many ice cubes dropping into ma glass scrambles his answer. "Sorry, hen, I missed that."

"They didn't know they had a problem. They checked the logs, saw the tech comment, assumed that maintenance had been overzealous. They scheduled a replacement for the next day and it wasn't until the morning that maintenance called asking 'where's the train'.

"Don't trains have transponders like planes do?"

"This one was turned off, also pointing to an inside job."

"Well it can't get off the Victoria line," I start to say. His face says different.

"With enough knowledge you can stash a train anywhere on any line on the underground network. That nice clean tube map we see at every station looks nothing like the real thing. It doesn't even begin to cover the sidings and disused lines."

"Shite." I mutter, beginning to see the scale of his problem.

"I have a pretty long night ahead of me," Seb says. "I'll review the footage, but if the guy knew what he was doing he won't have left his face uncovered."

"Want some coffee before you go?" I ask, walking back from the kitchen.

"No thanks, I'm awash with the stuff." He goes into the bedroom and comes out wearing dark comfortable clothes.

"I can't bargain with Pond if I don't have the location of this train in my back pocket. I suppose I'd better get on with finding it."

"Break a leg," I say, blowing him a kiss. We don't wish each other luck any more. The last time we did that, Pond kicked him to the kerb.

CHAPTER 5

Without Seb in the flat it feels big and empty. It never used to. Before he moved in this place was my sanctuary, an escape from the world.

I'm not a natural sharer and even though I asked him to move in, it has still taken a while to get each other's rhythms. We've both had to make allowances: a cap left off the toothpaste, your partner claiming the side of the bed you used to sleep on, you grabbing the wrong razor in a steamy bathroom, and leaving him a sopping wet towel——all things you treat as quirks, not reasons to hold a grudge. And gradually your possessions start to mingle just as your personalities do. Without really planning to, we've passed the road sign that says 'now entering coupledom'.

Nights like this present a dilemma. Seb may be train hunting until the early hours. The old me would stay in and read. Or work on the fledgling short story I started writing at Seb's bedside while he was recovering from the gunshot wound and beating he'd sustained in the line of duty. The new me wants to go out and catch a show, or head up to one of the capital's hidden gem rooftop bars. I lock up and take myself off to one of the less touristy karaoke bars Seb has introduced me to.

One Cuban sandwich and a dram later, the singers are warming up. We just had two merry office workers leaning back to back whilst belting out Bon Jovi's, 'Livin' on a Prayer'. The familiar chords of the next song pull me back to just after the end of the Gnomen Pearson affair.

Summer 2006

Seb and I crashed through the door of a little dive bar. It was our third date night after moving in together and it had just begun sheeting down with rain. We weren't the only ones caught without an umbrella and we ducked into the first place we came to. Seb's shirt was almost transparent, my suit sodden.

The place stank of roll-ups, old spice and CAMRA members, but it also had a gas fire going full tilt. Oh the joys of London in the Summer. I parked myself next to it while Seb got a couple of drams and, wonder of wonders, a towel from the barman. An aging jukebox was on autoplay; the rattle and clack as each vinyl plate was selected, the mechanical 'pop' as the needle dropped onto the disc, and the hiss, like steam on ice. I told Seb about my da's expensive old Bang and Olafson record player with the diamond stylus and the ten pence pieces we used to balance on the head of the arm to extend the life of the needle, and how mad da used to get when he caught us doing that.

Slipping my jacket off I draped it over the back of a nearby chair. Apart from a dopey golden lab and his owner, silently sleeping in the booth beside him with his head back, mouth open, a pair of flies buzzing lazily around his nose, the place was empty. Seb and I talked, our voices quiet. Waves of heat from the gas fire were drying our clothes. Seb's shirt crackled as he moved. Running my fingers over the material it felt rough, unfinished. Every few records we moved our chairs further from the fire; the heat that close becoming unbearable. We drained our glasses and Seb took them back over to the bar.

As the opening chords of Spandau Ballet's 'True' crossed the room so did he, taking my hand, drawing me upright, his arms enfolded me. I pressed my body against his chest, then reached up, resting both forearms on his collar bones and cupped the back of his neck with my palms and fingertips. The skin back there felt like the material of his shirt. Seb rested his face close to mine, holding me gently but firmly around the waist. His kiss, inevitable. Seb's kiss made my blood feel fizzy and my world shrink to the man in front of me. I wanted to breathe him in, stay joined forever at the lips.

"Love?" a woman's voice is coming from directly in front of me. "You with us?"

A slight tremor runs through my body, yanking me back to the present where a harassed looking waitress has a hand on my forearm.

"Sorry, I was miles away."

"Well I didn't think it was 'is singing that put a look like that on your face." She gestures with her head towards the young guy weaving his way past us. Bohemian Rhapsody, which is almost an anthem for this place, is now playing. Anyone can and is joining in via the mics at their tables.

I laugh, she places a full glass of champagne in front of me.

"From the hoorays over there," she answers my questioning look by pointing towards the bar. The group, Oxbridge types, chinless wonders the lot of them. Between them their parents probably own most of the home counties. "They think you look lonely and they didn't tell me to say that." She pushes a bunch of stray blonde hairs back behind one metal clad ear. "They're dropping money like it's going out of fashion."

The song has reached the stage where Queen 'just wanna get out, just wanna get right out of here' and I'm with them. I pull out a twenty from my wallet and hand it to the girl, "For any trouble they give you."

She tucks the note into her bra and gives me a conspiratorial wink. Like a Mexican wave, patrons are getting to their feet to give the last part of the song some wellie.

Now pictures of me wouldn't frighten small children but there's a reason the hoorays picked me. A woman alone, even a woman older than them, easy prey. There's a twiglet of mini-skirted Essex twenty somethings to their left who practically have their tongues hanging out over the bar, but while men can hunt in packs, packs of women still intimidate them.

Guys who treat women like possessions are guys I have no wish to be around, and Seb has given me some useful little tools to improve my self-defense arsenal. Luckily, tonight, I don't need to use them.

Arriving back around 11:30, no sign of Seb. I take a book to bed and doze off with the light still on.

I start awake. My mobile is ringing and I grab it. I know it isn't Seb, his ringtone is the Ipcress File theme.

"'Ello?"

"Mary, this is Daz. Oh, did I wake you?"

"Aye you woke me, hen. It's the back o' midnight."

"Can you come? Quick."

CHAPTER 6

Daz said to meet him at Victoria Station, I put on a tracksuit over my pjs and a hooded raincoat because it is hissing it down again outside. The sense of urgency in Daz's voice propels me out of the flat and onto the street. It takes only a few minutes to get to the station. The grey steel shutters are pulled across. No sign of Daz in Terminus Place, but his motorcycle, a dark blue Triumph Tiger, is across the street, chained to the railings next to the statue of mounted Marshal Foch.

I take out my phone and call him.

"Daz?"

"I'm inside," his voice is hushed. "Tug the shutter."

To humour him I do, and it slides a little to the left. Peeping through at me is Daz.

I slide past him and he pulls the barrier closed again. The station concourse is full lit and deserted. It is a curious feeling looking at the whole area without it being broken up by people. The departure boards are all blank and you could eat your dinner off the floors.

"You can go in," Daz says from behind me. "All the cameras are switched off."

"You guessing, hen?"

"I swear on the blood of my ancestors."

Keeping my hood up, I inspect the nearest camera. He's right, the red light is out.

I try to grab hold of his arm. "What are you up to, Daz?"

"I," he slips past me and walks towards the entrance to the tube, imbuing his chat with the same urgency that got me down here, "have still been looking for the guy who rescued me, London's version of Batman. This wasn't just a one off. When I started to look I found plenty of stories about him on the internet. I want to do my own story."

I cover my alarm with a liberal dose of sarcasm. "Since when did you start covering the crime beat, hen?"

"I'm doing this in my spare time."

"You think he's down *there*?" We've stopped at the top of the stairs leading into the underground; a position which would get us trampled underfoot if the station were open.

"No." For once Daz seems unable to marshal his facts. "I was hanging around out there. He seems to operate around this area. I didn't find him but I did see something very weird."

"This is London hen, you'll have to define weird."

Again the false start and a little stuttering, not from nerves. His eyes are shining with journalistic fervor.

"Look, it would be better to show you." He trots down the stairs. "Are you coming?"

"Ooch no. I'm nae going there, not without a dirty great torch, hen."

"We won't need one."

He is now past the metal gate that always makes me think of sheep waiting to be dipped. It leads down stairs protected with doc martin style steel toe caps into the ticket hall.

He keeps moving downwards. I could walk away back to ma nice warm bed. Muttering an oath I follow him.

If it was unsettling seeing the station concourse sans people, standing in the middle of the ticket hall triples the creepy factor. The lighting down here is always dim. My da, who instilled the idea of using public transport wherever possible, likens this area to an ants nest. A constant flow of stinking silent humanity he called it. It always smells of salt and vinegar down here, interspersed with lethal doses of hairspray and aftershave that could gas a woman at fifty paces. Without the flapping of coats and the eddys and currents of bodies in motion, the air in here is still and jungle humid.

The ticket barriers are, of course, the only things working. Daz takes a few steps back and launches himself over the nearest one, grazing his behind on the top of the barrier, causing him to stumble-run comically to a halt. With a sigh I take out my wallet and let the equipment scan my Oyster. I pass through the gates and join a slightly winded Daz.

"You're arm's better then," I say.

"Why did you do that? If they check your Oyster they'll see you were here in the middle of the night."

"You've been watching C.S.I again, haven't you, hen? The only reason anyone would bother to check ma card is if they think I've been fare dodging, do I look like a fare dodger to you?"

"What does a fare dodger look like?" Daz counters.

"Who is down there? Tell me now or I'm away to ma bed, Daz."

"The paper has a tips line. All the big ones do. We got one today that said something odd was going down at Victoria Tube station tonight. I arranged to meet the guy here over an hour ago but he never showed. I'd just unchained my bike and was about to call it a night when this big black anonymous transit van pulled up outside. I hid behind the statue and watched. Men got out, all in black, ninja style. I'd classify that as odd. Van drives off. Two railway employees, walkie-talkies and hi-vis vests let them into the station entrance. I re-chained the bike and nipped across the road. The lead ninja was telling them to deactivate the cameras; he didn't want himself or his men on film. They clumped down here and I followed. They went that way," he points towards the Piccadilly line. "I went down and had a listen. The yellow vests led them to platform 2 and from there into the tunnel."

I'm thinking we should turn around. Daz's insatiable curiosity will be fired up if he learns anything about a missing tube train and I have no wish to possibly come across Seb with Daz in tow.

I'm saved from having to make the decision when voices and some mouth-watering scents carry along the corridor. Daz mutters something food related and suddenly, out of nowhere I'm dying for a kebab. We can hear at least four people. A couple of those voices heavy with strain. "Keep your end up," one of them, complains. "I don't want this bugger falling off."

Daz stands there with his ears cocked. I'm pretty sure if I hadn't grabbed a handful of his good arm and yanked on it, he would've been waiting to greet the unknowns, up to god knows what. I use the Oyster and tow the two of us through. I can hear him legging it up the stairs behind me. As it is we barely make it out into the dreich. We slide the shutter completely closed, race across the street, and press ourselves into the concrete base of the statue, before the men yank the shutter back open again. Two of them are man-handling a stretcher.

"A body," Daz says into my ear, making me jump.

Even though we're getting drenched, we keep our vantage point. Both of us are wearing dark clothing so we shouldn't be noticed. The same (presumably) black panel van pulls up and they load the stretcher into the back. Two of the men get in with it. The hi-vis vest guys shamble off into the rain, I wonder if they're going to warm up in the back alley dive Seb sometimes drinks at. Beside me, chains clink as Daz once again frees his bike from the railings.

"Where do you think you're going, hen?" I ask, as he takes the Tiger off of its kick stand. "Your arm."

Daz straddles the thing and stamps down to bring the engine to life. "After them," he yells over the rasping engine. "The arm is fine. Batman can wait. This is a story I can totally get my teeth into!" He crams the open face helmet onto his head, does up the strap, and pulls the goggles over his eyes. "You coming?"

"Nae. I've done enough daft things for one night."

"See you at the park tomorrow, gelati!" and he kicks the Tiger forward, roaring off into the rain; keeping the headlight off so that by the time the big bike catches up to the van turning up ahead, he's virtually invisible to the driver. Hopefully he'll have the good sense not to get himself hurt. I've given up trying to tell people I care about what's good for them. I'm nae exactly a shining example of common sense myself.

Back at the flat I stand under the jets of the shower for a good ten to fifteen minutes, letting the water pummel my muscles and warm up my body. Before showering I stuck a couple of big bath towels in the dryer to warm them up. Wrapped in warmth from head to toe I crawl into bed.

***

I'm on the stairs, alone. Victoria Underground is lit up like one of the Christmas display windows at Selfridges. Baggy grey overalls, a head mounted flashlight, on my feet knee high wellies. I call Daz's name a few times before moving down the stairs. I'm in a white bathroom-style tiled corridor following the signs towards the platforms when the lights dip. It happened so fast that maybe I imagined it. I take another step, and another, and another. Now I know I didn't imagine it; the lights are getting fractionally dimmer and dimmer like a permanent brown out. Try as I might, I can't turn around and walk away.

Just as I set foot on Platform 2 they fail completely. True darkness is more like a dark wind. You can't see. I mean total nothingness. I've been in an underground cave in the Peak District where they flipped off the lights for a couple of seconds; it felt like hours, not seconds. The guide cheerfully informed us, after flipping on the lights, that in a very short time in total darkness you could go insane. Straining not to panic, I fumble with the head mounted torch. Its beam spears the darkness; then it too starts to flicker and goes out. I keep my feet moving. My chest, my breath, compress. A surge of panic drowns out anything else. Every step could be the one that pitches me off the platform.

A strange low pitched drone, part hum, part whistle, that has been background noise, gets louder and louder. The darkness is pressing down on me, sucking my breath from my body. I lift my foot and it lands on solid ground. I let myself fall backwards; the platform absorbs my fall. I flip over and start to crawl back down the platform toward the exit. Dream logic: if I move away the lights might come back on. The unearthly whistle becomes a roar. A vacuum drags me back towards the invisible mouth of the tunnel. My feet go over the edge the point of no return. I'm falling. The roar rises to ear splitting levels and the darkness is torn apart. So am I.

"Arrrrrgh, noooooooooooooo!"

Breathless, panicked, the dark, the platform, the tube train bearing down on me. There's something on my face. I claw it back and something snags both wrists. I break the grip the way Seb taught me, and open hand the air, connecting with warm skin. There's a solid thump and I open my eyes.

The thing on my face was the bedsheet and the grip came from Seb who is lying winded beside the bed.

"Uhhhhh."

He's the one lying on the floor. He's the one I just whacked. The first thing he says is, "Are you okay?"

I get my breath back, shake my head.

"Bad dream." I flop back onto the pillow. "I belted you, hen. Sorry."

"I see you've got the wrist lock-break I showed you, down." He struggles up and sits on the edge of the bed. "I came out of the shower and you were thrashing about, your mouth was wide open. I was trying to calm you down when you lashed out. That was a pretty good tap to the jaw."

I don't correct him.

He's been teaching me the basics of Krav Maga the self-defense technique the Israelis teach their security forces. I asked him to after I got attacked in my flat last year when I only survived because I had a makeshift weapon, a healthy dose of luck, and my opponent was a dunderheid.

We spar some mornings if there's time. And he gives me home work; the wrist lock-break for instance. "I have a good teacher," I say, not wanting to put any more dents in his pride.

"As long as you're not going to start ambushing me around the apartment like Cato."

As a break from all those magic shows, I dragged him to a Pink Panther retrospective at the Electric in Notting Hill one Sunday last month. He still has Cato Fong on his mind.

"I can promise you that," I say, sneezing.

"Bless you! Are you coming down with something?"

"Was out in the rain last night." Shite, I didn't mean to say that.

"So was I."

"Went to see that new movie over at the Leicester Square Odeon," I improvise. "Got soaked on the way back over."

He's giving me that look, the one which says he doesn't quite believe me, but he doesn't push it.

"Did you find your missing train?" I ask, getting out of bed and hunting for a clean tracksuit and socks.

"No, but we found the driver." He goes out to the kitchen and I follow him. "One Patrick Coltrane."

"What did he have to say?"

He pours me a cup of fresh brewed coffee, filling it to the brim. I take a sip and wince. Seb uses coffee like a vitamin and the stronger it is the better. This stuff could fray ma teeth. I pour some of it down the sink and add cold water.

"Not much. I'm attending his autopsy this morning."

I dilute the coffee a second time. Now at least it's sippable.

"We had to go in after hours to retrieve the body, Think crispy duck, <u>extra</u> crispy."

The slug of coffee halfway down my throat reverses course. I swallow hard to keep it down.

"Could the world of commerce spare you this morning?" Seb asks.

"After I've cleared my in tray, I have a whole butt load of nothing today. Why? Are you inviting me to an autopsy?"

"Well, yes. Pond's assigned me a small security detail of guys I don't know and therefore don't trust. Any of them."

That's a hard thing for Seb to admit. He *did* trust his fellow agents to the hilt, up until this summer when one of them betrayed him.

"I'd rather have someone trustworthy watching my back," he says.

"Careful hen, your paranoia's showing," I tease. "Besides if anything kicks off all I can do is yell 'look out' really loud. My self-defense works one on one as in I can defend me. You kept me away from the arcane stuff, remember?"

He tries one more time, "You did sign the official secrets act."

"Well, it was that or get free room and board at Paddington Green nick courtesy of the anti-terror mob. It wasn't something I *wanted* to do. Pond didn't give me any choice. And, for the record, it's something I regret doing more every day." I lace up my trainers and, keeping my gaze on the floor, say, "I think I'll take a rain check and keep my breakfast where it belongs."

"Heading to the park?"

"Yes, it's my Tuesday morning jog meeting with Daz."

Seb and I leave the flat together. He walks towards the tube. While jogging towards the park I wonder, if we had stayed at the top of the stairs last night, would we have seen him coming up from the tunnels below.

Daz made a comment last night that didn't register then. It comes roaring back to me now. *"Where did they lay hands on pulled-pork at this time of night?"*

Or crispy duck, <u>extra</u> crispy. The fact that the smell that set my mouth watering could've been from another human being makes me want to boke in the bushes. I whoosh in some big deep breaths until the feeling passes. I let the guilt ease up and start to jog, looking for Daz. One whole circuit later there's bin no sign of him. With leg muscles mildly complaining, I jog over to the café we use, buy two coffees, park my arse on a seat, and call him.

"Hello?" The word is muffled, like he's got a hand over the microphone.

"Daz, I'm at the park. Where are you?"

"I'm still following the van."

"Still? You haunting a morgue or something, hen?"

"No, I'm in a disused warehouse in Docklands, and *I'm not alone.*"

Well that explains the whispering. "Any idea where in Docklands?"

"No. The van's parked out front, engine running. They're waiting for something. Not sure what."

Or who, I think.

"Oi!" Someone on Daz's end yells. I hear a curse in Indian, the scuffles of someone running. Daz's phone cuts off.

CHAPTER 7

"Daz!" Several of the café's patrons are staring at me.

I curse up a silent blue streak. I've tried to cut down on the swearing since moving into my da's office. Now it would be just my luck to have a fellow jogger recognize me and skewer me in 140 characters or less.

Daz is no helpless bairn. He can take care of himself. Except he may have waded into something far over his head. I have only a rough idea of his location. Saying he's in the 'undeveloped district' is like throwing a needle into thin air and hoping it hits a haystack. I've got two hours before I need to be at my desk. I sprint back towards the office. Having learned my lesson with cars, I've bought myself a non-descript emergency vehicle, an old primer gray

Ford Focus. It sits taxed and insured and with a full tank of petrol on the lower level of Maccallans underground car park. I give Seb a call before pulling into traffic.

"Hey, I've changed my mind. If you need my help I'm offering, hen."

"You'll have to be quick. We've got a bit of a situation here so I've had to move up the timetable. If you can get to the Victoria Docks in the next, say, twenty minutes, I should still be here."

"Victoria Docks." Seems all roads lead to Victoria these days. "I'm on my way."

"Call when you're close and I'll guide you in."

It's barely eight and the traffic congestion that would usually slow me up is mercifully absent. Oh there's traffic, it's just not behaving like a blocked waste disposal. The overcast morning is a hangover from last night's downpour. Just after entering the Victoria Docks area I pull over, turn the headlights off, and call Seb again.

"I'm still a ways away, hen."

Then I see him. He's striding round the corner the next street over.

"I'll be gone by the time you get here, Mary. You might as well turn around and go back."

He vanishes back behind a disused warehouse, still talking to me.

"Okay, hen. Sorry tae have messed you about."

"No problem. I'll be out for the rest of the day. Call you when I get back?"

"Aye."

Still wondering where he's going, I hear and feel the rumble of a container lorry passing my parked car.

"Bye, hen."

I pull out the ignition key, shut the door and arm the alarm using the key fob. At the corner of the warehouse I stop and take a careful nosy round the corner. The lorry, which I'd assumed was full of frozen goods on their way to some supermarket or other has parked; the back doors are open and a ramp extends down to the tarmac. The van that Daz and I saw last night is in the process of driving up that ramp. Seb must be inside because there's no sign of him on the street. There's a lazy breeze cutting across the back of my neck. I turn my collar up to my ears.

Having eaten the van, the container lorry retracts the ramp and a man gets out of the front cab. He has

HMSS written all over him. I pull back around the corner because with his gimlet peepers he's gonna see me. Once the truck has pulled away, I give it a few more minutes to leave the scene completely and then go around to the side of the warehouse. It is in a right sorry state: one door hanging off, only propped up by a stack of metal shipping containers, the stink of diesel and damp, the concrete floor pitted and buckled. Oiled shoe prints lead out of the mouth of the warehouse and away towards the van. An oiled single tire track does the same.

'Snobs Go Home' has been spray-painted across the other door and the inside wall, along with 'Jobs Not Snobs'. Royal Victoria Docks, along with the Isle of Dogs, is next on the developer's hit list. They claim to be gentrifying the docks, but bringing white collar jobs like banking and tech to an area where the closest residents are working class doesn't sit well with me. The blocks of luxury apartments going up are already attracting people who work out towards Canary Wharf. Property taxes are going up as a result——Snobs go home indeed. London didn't need a new financial centre, the developers did.

"Daz?" I call, cupping my hands to keep my voice from carrying too far. "It's me. It's Mary. They've gone. You can come out now, hen."

All I get is a bunch of startled pigeons rising into the rafters, like an el cheapo action scene in a cut-price John Woo movie.

I venture further in, calling Daz's name. The fumes are getting stronger. My trainers squelch on oil and old tyre marbles and my eyes start to water.

"Daz!"

Finally he appears, filthy.

"Those devils took my bike," he complains. "How did you find me?" I can see suspicion brewing in his head like clouds bubbling up over an open plain.

"Let's talk when we're out of here." I hate myself a little at this point because to distract Daz means putting this on him. "What have you gotten yourself into, hen?" I hurry him out of the warehouse and over to my car. "I turned in here and pulled over to try and call you." Briefly I summarize the panel van being driven up the ramp into the trailer.

"Which way did they go?"

"Don't know, and I don't think they'll be back. Unless they're keen on finding you." I ramp up the sarcasm, because I can see he's thinking again. He arranges himself in the car.

"Seatbelt," I say, clipping my own and waiting for him to do the same. "We'll go a different way back in case your friends are waiting at the roundabout up there." I'm trailing a lorry, hoping that I don't end up driving onto a building site.

"I've never seen this car before. Is it yours?"

"Aye, I have to use a car occasionally, hen, and this one blends in better than my da's Merc."

"It's automatic," he says, making that sound like a terrible disease.

My phone rings. Even though using a hands free kit is legal, I try not to take business calls on the road. I check the digital clock on the dashboard, just past nine o'clock. Jo will be wondering where the heck I am.

"Jo?"

"No, it's Seb. Can you talk?"

"Not really, I'm still in the car." He knows this means I'm on speakerphone because I refuse to wear one of those Bluetooth ear pieces. "I'm saving the company money by picking up a client from the Docklands airport."

"We waited as long as we could. I'm pretty well gone for the day now. Are you free for dinner tonight?"

"Aye, hen."

"Tony's. Pick you up at eight?"

"Aye."

Seb rings off.

"Your intended?" Daz fractures the last word into three crisp syllables.

"My boyfriend," I correct him. "And you shouldn't be concerning yourself with ma dating life when you don't have one of your own. Or do you?"

Here, surprisingly, Daz mirrors his father. He seems to even relish the arrangements his father has made. "A politician's daughter, well versed in the 'womanly arts'."

This makes me snort.

"You don't approve?"

"It's none of my business," I say, wishing the lights ahead would go green. "I prefer to choose my own partner. Having a man tell me what to do would do ma heid in."

"I cannot imagine anyone telling you what to do."

"You've no met ma da, hen. He tries to do that all the time."

"I am quite sure that those discussions are...spirited." Daz says. "My bride to be comes from means and is spirited in her own right. The two of you would get along; of that I am sure."

"Do me a favour, hen. Don't crush that spirit."

I pull the car into our underground car park, click the locks, and usher Daz into the lift. Arriving outside the reception area, I can hear Jo's staccato taps on the keyboard. When she gets into that rhythm I have to close my office door. Otherwise the sound can become hypnotic.

"Hello Jo, sorry I'm late. I had to go and retrieve Mr. Patel."

Jo gives me one of her looks. She doesn't say anything though.

"Could you pop down to the canteen and get us a pot of coffee and some biscuits?"

Jo gets up and heads for the canteen, I take Daz into my office, closing the door behind us.

He has an interesting take on the container lorry.

"Mobile morgue," he says, slipping off his coat. I'm pleased to see that the bandage has gone and the jagged map on his arm is fading though smudged with dirt containing god knows what. I toss Daz the wet wipes I keep in my office drawer. He whisks several out of the pack and dabs frantically at his arm until the muck has gone. "It's not an unfamiliar concept. They used refrigerated trucks to preserve the dead from the Twin Towers so that they could identify them. My friend is a photographer. He has pictures of those trucks lined up a few streets away from the scene. I smell a government conspiracy."

"Pretty big leap, hen."

"You tell me." Daz lays his digital tape recorder down on my desk and presses play.

His voice is the first I hear. Even hushed, the excitement crackles.

"I've been following the black panel truck seen outside Victoria station since last night. It is now six a.m. I've been in on foot. The truck is parked in front of a run-down warehouse in Docklands. There is a side entrance. I'll push my bike in through there."

There's a double click, almost a scratch, as Daz pauses and then unpauses the recording. I briefly picture myself back on campus, pacing my dorm, thoughts in head, microcassette recorder in hand doing exactly the same thing. The recorder clicks back on.

"Six nineteen." We listen to Daz's breathing for a few minutes. "Oi!" Scuffling sounds. Daz shakes his head as if to say not me.

"Hold still, I'm not going to hurt you. What are you doing in here?"

"I was sleeping." It's a different voice, one that sounds like a pre hypothermic Marvin the paranoid android. "Just minding me own business." A sly note enters his voice. "I know I'm not s'posed to be here, but I've been lying here awake for a while and you aren't supposed to be here either. You're filth aren't ya?" Another pause. "I can shuffle off for a bit if one of you...". He leaves the rest unsaid.

The first voice and another one can be heard in a muffled, whispered argument.

"I've only got a tenner," says one.

"Give him that then. The smallest I've got is a twenty," the other retorts. Marvin solves the problem with a giant sigh, and whether he took the ten or the twenty, we both can hear a note being crumpled.

"Thanks boys. How long should I be gone?"

More whispers and the reply? "A couple of hours should do it."

"I'll be at the transport caff down the way. Don't touch my sleeping bag or any of my stuff."

One man grumbles. The other tells him to put in an expense claim. After a few more minutes of silence, Daz whispers, "Six thirty-five."

Clearly the two men who rousted the homeless chap have no idea they're being overheard.

"We found the driver, so why can't we find the train?" says the one who only had a tenner.

Now my ears prick up. How many missing trains can there be?

"Why aren't we sweating the driver? What's his name, Trick Coltrane? What kind of a name is Trick?"

"Short for Patrick, and he's dead. The third rail saw him off."

"Christ, what a way to go!"

A sharp double beep interrupts them. "Message from the guv'nor. He's five minutes out."

"What's he like, Miller? I've never worked with him before."

"Sandringham type, but solid. Worked on that big gangster op. Got himself injured, earned some brownie points by saving the Chief's life."

I very nearly mutter 'bloody cheek' out loud. Seb was too busy bleeding to do any saving. That was down to me. Something else I regret doing.

"I heard he got suspended by medical. How come he's fronting this op?"

"Chief's been throwing the poor bastard scraps."

"This is a lot more than scraps," the other man says. "Heads up, I hear a car." The engine dies, a door slams. I can picture Seb walking towards the men. A scrabbling noise coming from very close to the recorder. I look questioningly at Daz.

"I was trying to get into a better position. Then you called and even though my ringer was off they must've heard."

"You're lucky they didn't catch you."

"I ran towards the side door and then doubled back and hid in a stack of pipes, unlit. They didn't even try and climb to the top of the stack like I did. It was a gamble but it paid off. They left with my bike. I don't know how long it was before you turned up. It felt like hours."

He stands up pacing my office. "Those men. I've been thinking they could be Special Branch or security services."

"Whoever they are, they can ID you now."

"They only have my bike. I registered it under a false name."

He sounds so proud of himself, they could arrest him just for that.

"And what a story. A missing train!"

"Slow down Daz. If, and it's a pretty big if, those men *were* Special Branch, they won't take kindly to you letting it be known that TFL lost a train. Don't they have C notices; I mean D notices for stuff at your paper they want kept secret?"

"It's just a train. It can't have gone far."

Not true, I think, but don't say.

"Maybe," he says, more to himself than me. "Maybe it's not the train itself but the passengers, or the train had something of value stashed on board."

"Supposition, as my lawyer uncle would say."

Daz stops in mid-pace. "I have to find the train before Special Branch or anyone else does!" he says, face flushed in triumph. "Once I find it, I can demand an exclusive in exchange for the vehicle location!"

"Daz, there are miles of tunnels down there, most of them electrified. You heard what happened to Coltrane, the driver." I'm voicing genuine concern.

Far from putting Daz off from becoming an underground train spotter, he's now pursuing the idea with renewed vigor.

"And don't forget the tube trains could mow you down like a fly on a windscreen. And you'd be trespassing." That last reason sounds lame, but it could be enough to land Daz in jail. "Also, the real maps are probably under lock and key in a railway museum somewhere."

"Then it's a good job that my great, great grandfather was part of the team that documented the original underground network when it was being built. I'd bet my Porsche on there being disused lines or even a ghost station close to Victoria."

He bounds around the desk and gives me a hug as I get up from my chair. "Thanks for the save, gelati."

"Please be careful," I say. "Remember your spirited bride to be. I'm sure she wants you all in one piece."

CHAPTER 8

There's muffled shouting coming from the outer office followed by a 'thud' against my door. I go to check the source and Jo nearly joins me in my office.

"What's going on, Jo?"

"These gentlemen are here to evacuate us and they won't tell me why. I was trying to get some answers when he," she indicates an older man in a brown suit, "tried to barge his way into your office."

I've seen empire builders before, they call them Jobsworths down south as in 'it's more than my job's worth'.

"Is there a fire?" I address the man who isn't Jobsworth, over Jo's shoulder. "I didn't hear an alarm."

"We've detected unexploded ordinance, WWII era." Jobsworth replies with a bunch of words a wee girl wouldn't understand. I'm no a wee girl.

"German?"

"Yes."

"Did you say there's a UXB nearby?" Daz is craning his neck at the window. "Bomb disposal trucks are pulling up. You can see the yellow stripe across the top and down the side. Is the UXB live?" he asks.

Jobsworth almost genuflects. "We don't know sir, but you and your staff need to get out of here. UXB's are usually 500 lbs. If it went off, and it still could even after all these years, it would clear an area of roughly 400 square feet. They'd be picking us up with tweezers, sir."

I walk to the fire alarm and set it off. As it wails, I grab all the important documents out of the safe and stuff them into my gym bag. It smarts that Jobsworth thinks Daz is my boss so I cut him out of our conversation by forming a triangle between me, Daz, and Jo, leaving him gaping like a just landed trout.

As well as being our first aider, Jo is the Fire Marshall.

"Jo, go to the muster point and take a head count. Then send everyone home. First check their contact details, just in case."

"Where are you going?" she asks, as she sweeps the two men out of the way and opens her desk drawer for her handbag and her emergency drill clipboard.

"To check the boardroom. You know they ignore fire drills. If any of the MAC gets blown up the old bastards might try haunting me."

"The MAC?" Daz pants, as we pelt down the corridor.

"Mary Anning collection."

"Still none the wiser."

The boardroom is empty. I take a quick detour up to my flat and stuff some clothes into my gym bag. Then we run down the backstairs and out to the muster point where Jo and Jobsworth are waiting for us.

"All personnel have been evacuated," Jo says to me.

Over our heads, the steady clip clop of rotor blades. Looking back from the other side of the police barrier, we watch as a fleet of helicopters lower giant white balloon shaped objects. They vanish behind Maccallans HQ.

"Sandbags," Daz says into my ear. "They're playing it clever. Sand will absorb some of the blast, damp sand will absorb even more."

I give him a questioning look.

"I wrote my thesis on the history of UXB's during WWII. It's one of the reasons I chose London for my internship."

Behind us another bomb disposal unit van with that distinctive yellow stripe Daz was talking about parks. We get moved farther back behind another set of hastily put up police barriers. I leave Seb a voice message. Daz takes out his press credentials and walks towards a knot of policemen. He got an exclusive, just not the one he thought he was going to get.

As for me there's nae much I can do. And our employees get the rest of the day off.

The bomb squad works at defusing the bomb, whilst tourists vie for a glimpse of them from behind police barriers. The whole thing will be the lead story on tonight's six o'clock news. In the meantime, I walk over to Hyde Park, stake claim to a bench, and make a long phone call to Bangalore.

As the afternoon wears on the news only gets worse, and this is straight from the horse's mouth news. The police aren't talking to *anybody*. The workmen, oh they're talking plenty. I rented the first P.O. box I came to just off Whitehall and stashed the contents of the safe inside. Walking around carrying a gym bag overflowing with papers was attracting attention, and not the good kind.

Then I nosey around. The workmen are coming out of the site on the far side. They are rotating three crews every thirty minutes. One lot digs, the next lot sits in a staging area behind the police cordon, and the lot who have just dug get time to get food and drink. Having worked out where they are, and that they're somewhat ticked off, I go and raid the nearest M&S.–Loaded down with two bags of ready-mades and a selection of apples, bananas, and copious amounts of chocolate, I greet the next bunch of hungry diggers.

I've fought off randy drunken Glaswegians during Prom night; this should be a wee doddle.

"I'm from the council. This is the best I could do so far," I say, bustling up to the group of ten dirt caked workers. "I've got a coffee urn coming, but for now this should tide ye over."

I call up the company we use for catering and secure a large urn as well as a bloke called Fizal, who'll be in charge of operating it.

When they aren't stuffing their faces with sandwiches the men are talking. I can't help but listen to the many different points of view.

"We don't even know if it's a present from jerry. The foreman saw metal where there wasn't supposed to be any and panicked," says one.

"I heard the foreman's likely to be sacked. The bosses wanted to cover up the whole thing literal like."

"It's been in the ground for years. Didn't those things have clockwork fuses that'll be rotted into oblivion by now?"

"They 'ad all sorts of fuses. If they dropped it on London and it didn't go off it might not be a clockwork fuse. My father in law, 'is dad worked as a UXB technician. Them bombs were always changin'. Booby trapped some of 'em, and the worse ones 'e said were the ones they dropped and days later the buggers exploded with no warnin' at all. Evil bastards."

"The fuse isn't the problem. Whatever explosives the thing is packed with are the problem. They could be inert or they could be so unstable that a simple sneeze sets them off."

"That military bod, making us give up our phones, saying they might set off the bomb. Load of bollocks that is if you ask me."

"They don't want us taking pictures, plain and simple, and if they'd said that; been honest with us like... I mean, they kicked that Paki reporter off the site just for asking a sensible question about shutting down traffic."

"He was Indian you muppet..."

The electric coffee urn arrives at this point. I back off and let Fizal get on with it. He manages to sweet talk the closest shop owner into letting him plug the urn in. When I get back with more sandwiches and some cash for Fizal from the ATM machine next to M&S, the next lot have arrived and are supping away. The conversation is more of the same and I don't learn anything new, except they're now sure it's a UXB. They've evacuated Buckingham Palace, purely as a precaution, and the changing of the guard is cancelled until further notice.

The next lot out are the last for now. The excavation has uncovered the UXB and the bomb disposal people have moved in.–All unnecessary personnel have been dismissed.

"We've dug 'em a trench, cos the fuse part is facing down. Some poor sod's got to wriggle into that tiny trench on 'is back in one of them bulky bomb suits. And the trench is slap bang in the middle of a tiny tributary that wasn't on the map so they 'ave to keep pumping it awt so's 'e doesn't drown. I dunno about you, but I think I'd rather be without the suit. If that thing goes off it's what? 500llbs of highly unstable explosive? Goodnight Vienna either way."

"Hey council lady, woss yer name?"

"Mary." Damn. None of the others have asked ma name. For the surname, I use the rather squashed teacake he pulls from his pocket for inspiration, a snowball. "Mary Snow."

"Thanks for feeding us Mary Snow. Will you be 'ere tomorrow?"

"Er, I dunno. They wanted a volunteer and for me it was this or more filing."

Behind him the others are leaving.

That evening

When Seb surfaced he was tired. I suggested putting off our dinner tonight.

"Nonsense," he said over the phone. "I'm starving and I smell rank. I'll shower here after I've called Tony at the restaurant to make sure he's outside the blast cordon. If you don't hear from me I'll see you there at half past eight."

I get to Tony's half an hour early. I still have some clothes stored in the flat Seb sometimes uses. Tony embraces me with the usual 'mwah, mwah' on each cheek.

"Of course you can go up to the flat," he says.

It feels strange to be climbing these stairs again. The last time I was here, I was hiding from Gnomen Pearson, venturing out in disguise and stirring up a heap of trouble for Arthur Pond. The place looks exactly the same. I knew I didn't have a dress here, just a couple of M&S shirts I'd wear to the office. I exchange the zip-up tracksuit top and oil stained trainers for a form fitting shirt and a pair of ballet flats. I keep the navy lycra over my arm. It'll get much colder later.

I'm not the only one early. Downstairs Seb is already seated poring over his phone. Tony whips the wine glass out of the way as Seb reaches for water without looking.

I reach across and turn Seb's face away from the phone. Our lips meet; I feel his curve upwards. His hand comes to cup my cheek. We break and I sit down next to him.

"Sorry, Mary. I thought I could get this done before you got here. As soon as the antipasti arrives I'll shut it off, I promise."

"Still no sign of your missing?" We're both guarding our words because, unlike 'Nonna night' which has been moved to Mondays, most of the patrons within earshot of our table have full command of their English.

"Engine?" Seb offers, giving me a rueful smile. "I've got teams going over the disused and discontinued lines and so far, no luck."

He puts his phone on silent and places it under a snow white napkin where it buzzes with an incoming message. He looks across the table. The waiters place plates, dishes and sauces around us, with practiced ease.

"I'll ask Tony if we can sleep here tonight," Seb says, chasing an olive across the plate with his fork. "It's either that or try and find a hotel."

"I've never been evacuated before," I say, as I signal the waiter for a top up on my wine. "Might have to set up a temporary HQ. This isn't going to be over in a day."

"You know something I don't?" Even he can hear the words came out sharper than he intended. "Sorry Mary. Didn't mean to snap. It's been one of those days."

I bring him up to date on what I overheard.

"Hmm, the Mayor was busy down playing the whole thing on the radio earlier. He called the devices 'incendiaries'."

"That floppy haired twit." I notice my voice gets a little loud, must be the wine. "Honestly Seb, the lovable buffoon act works fine as a guest on 'Have I Got News for You'; in charge of running a city as big as this, nae so much."

"He is a political animal. He'll do his best not to shut down the city."

"You didn't hear the workmen, and I quote, 'One slip and its goodnight Vienna.'"

Dessert arrives: islands of espresso flavoured meringue floating in pools of Tony's home-made Nutella. I take a couple of mouthfuls. The entry bell rings and I look up out of habit; two coppers, accompanied by a suit. Seb follows my gaze and twists in his chair.

He turns back to me. "I know that bloke. He's Special Branch. Something's up."

No one else is paying them much attention as they vanish into the back. Seb drops his napkin on the table and scoops up his phone. "Back in a sec." He too enters the private area.

"Ladies and gents!" One of the policemen is standing by the door. "If you could make your way out of here in an orderly manner."

Seb still hasn't returned.

One of the diners, a pinstripe who could double for any of our board members, stands up and says, "I haven't finished or paid for my dinner." I mentally revise my opinion of him, upwards.

The suit from Special Branch emerges from the private area and says, "Sir, this is an evacuation.

Seb, not far behind him, reaches for my hand. Rather than be towed out, I pop one of the little meringues into my mouth, grab my jacket, and move away towards the exit. Without thinking about, it I've left Seb in my wake.

They direct us out onto Vauxhall bridge, into a stream of people crossing onto the other side of the Thames. I let people go past me until I'm level with Seb and the Special Branch suit.

"Two evacuations in one day, hen," I say to Seb. "What happened? That mythic UXB get bigger?"

Special branch shoots me a quizzical look.

"There's now more than one, Mary. Meet Oakes, he's a colleague. Oakes this is Mary Maccallan, my girlfriend."

"Charmed," says Oakes.

I do some rough calculations in my head. *Two* bombs? They've roughly doubled the blast radius,

Once all of us, Tony and staff included, are over the bridge and allegedly out of danger, I notice Tony going around making sure customers can get home. He flags down taxis for them and makes careful notes in his phone if a customer has concerns. His staff pile into another two taxis as Tony promises to keep them updated. He gives us a cheery wave as he walks off, still in his chef's whites. He is one of life's optimists.

"Don't worry about Tony. He's smart enough to come out the other side of this," Seb says. "Oakes, any idea how long this evacuation order is going to be in place?"

"Not a clue," he says, shifting from foot to foot. "I'm going back over, got to make sure that all the people are out."

He trudges back over the bridge, taking out his mobile phone as he walks away.

"We should start looking for a hotel room," I say. "And tomorrow I have to start looking for temporary office space. Me and the rest of the businesses in the area."

"Let me make a couple of calls before you do that," Seb says, slowing up and taking out his phone. I keep moving because I hate it when people hover around me when I'm making a call. I pass first time evacuees who are just milling about like a bunch of sheep. I stay in the main road so Seb doesn't have to hunt for me in side streets. Just past the MI6 building my phone makes the 'xylophone being dropped down a staircase' noise announcing a voicemail. A quick look at the screen shows me I have two, one from da and another from the head of our Spanish operation. They can both wait.

A cab cruises up alongside me. Seb sticks his head out of the window.

"I've found us a place for the night. Hop in."

CHAPTER 9

"Wandsworth?" Our cab is headed in that direction.

"Didn't know you were familiar," Seb says.

"Jo lives out this way, Wandsworth Common. We sometimes strategize at a café on the high street."

We seem to be heading that way. Then the cab turns off onto wide streets with towering old houses on either side; plenty of brick walls, high gates and other armour employed by the upper classes living amongst the plebs.

The taxi drops us one house from the end of the row. I count the stories as we walk up the path; five. And no telling if there's a basement too. Seb pays off the taxi, waits until he's gone, then makes another call.

"We're here," he says.

After a short delay we walk up the path. Seb takes out a key and unlocks the door. I take in the tiled front hall, the stairs that lead to the upper floors, and a glimpse of a large unlit room at the back.

"Why tell them you're here if you have a key?" I ask.

"Because I like to keep my head attached to my shoulders. The caretaker here can take care of himself."

"Care..." I don't get the chance to finish. The stairs shake to the treads of some very quick feet.

"Thanks for letting us stay here," Seb says to a pair of shoes that become legs that become an older man. Seb introduces 'Bernie.'

"Anything to help an old colleague," Bernie says when he's fully visible. He has a touch of the Anthony Hopkins about him; gimlet eyes, soft-ish vowels from the valleys, a lino ruck of wrinkles on his forehead. There the similarity ends. I don't think Sir Anthony would be caught dead in a lurid shirt of the Hawaiian variety teamed with a pair of tweed golf trousers. "Though I 'spose I'm the old colleague. Mary, we meet at last. I've heard Pond cursing you to high heaven young lady."

"Bernie retired a couple of months ago," Seb explains. "Six didn't want to lose him. Men like Bernie are hard to find. So he looks after this safe house for them."

"It's a nifty little deal," Bernie says. "I could never have stayed around the Capital on what my pension pays me. And I'm sure when Pond finds out I've let you two stay here he'll have a conniption."

At just gone ten neither Seb nor Bernie shows any inclination of being tired. I'm knackered but manage to hide my yawns.

Raising his glass of scotch my way, Seb asks, "How did you get the UXB information? The police wouldn't talk to anyone out of uniform, so what did you do?"

"I may have impersonated a council employee."

"D'you know how dangerous that could've been, sneaking onto a bomb site?"

"I wasn't on the site. I did a couple of circuits, found where the workmen were taking their breaks, and fed them. I was providing a public service."

"You were in the blast zone, Mary. If that bomb had gone off they would've..."

"...bin picking us up with tweezers, hen. Yes I heard that already." I wave away his concern with, "Have ya met me, hen. I'm not exactly risk averse. No one put a gun to ma heid and said 'feed those poor buggers'. And I didn't ask them questions. You lot are worse gossips that us when ya get goin. All I had to do was listen."

"You worry me sometimes, Mary. You're too much like..."

"Like who?"

"Forget it!" Seb necks his whiskey, puts his glass down, and stomps out of the back door.

"There's a big garden back there, it'll give him some time to cool off."

"I'm too much like who, Bernie?"

"Like his sister, Sandy."

"I remind him of his sister! That's..." He's drawn to me because I'm like his sister? "That's mingin'!"

"Oh you don't look like his sister. She's a stunner." He realizes his foot is planted in his mouth. "I mean, you're striking."

"Bernie, quit while you're aheid."

"Sandy's a bit of wild child. She's a smart cookie, little too smart for her own good. She's manipulative, and she fell in with the wrong crowd. Changed her name too, to Domino. Pond..." He breaks off the rest of whatever he was going to say because Seb re-appears, calmer than before. The night air pouring through the back door is alive with the rattle of the train tracks and the pop—pop of distant firecrack-ers.

Bernie shakes his head. "Not even November."

Later that night

"What's so funny?" Seb's voice comes out of the darkness as I slide back under the covers.

"I was just thinking of movie sex scenes," I mur-mur, "where everything is toned and airbrushed and no one has to go for a pee after."

He chuckles, the covers move, the mattress does a rusty mouse impression, and Seb snuggles up against my back. His arm burrows under my waist and joins up with the other one across my chest. The ring of warmth makes my head swim and I push my feet out of the bottom of the scratchy sheets to cool them.

The bedrooms in this safe house aren't exactly a suite at the Dorchester, or even the Travelodge. The sheets, though scratchy, are clean. The room's last occupant must have been here for a while; there's a dip in the middle of the bed that we both keep rolling into.

Early morning.

I've learned from previous experience that a drowsy, satiated Seb is more likely to engage in pillow talk, so before he can spoon me again the question slips out.

"Who's Domino?"

His immediate reaction is to unclamp my chest.

When he does speak, his voice is tight, on the verge of annoyed. "Bernie talks too much."

"You've been acting weird ever since I told you where I got my UXB information from."

"It's not the information. It's how you went about getting it. It's a bit Domino-esque. Mary, you bent the rules. That's the first step towards thinking rules aren't for you."

"I didn't do anything too illegal," I protest in a whisper.

"No but you walked into an area you knew to be dangerous. Domino once told me that she got a rush out of doing things like that."

I repeat my first question.

"Domino is my sister. The yin to my yang. I'm on one side of the law and she is on the other. I couldn't even try to recruit her because she got kicked out of St Hilda's for dealing weed. Because it was her 'first offence', well the first one she'd been caught doing, she got a fine and a bunch of unpaid hours working in the local old folk's homes, and that was it. As far as my parents were concerned she'd learned her lesson. She hadn't. She just got a hell of a lot more sneaky about covering her tracks. She was always brave; bungee jumping, solo backpacking, free climbing, and jumping out of airplanes, first with parachutes, and now, if the latest data is anything to go by, wingsuits."

"Is she a criminal?"

"Only by association so far. She hasn't done any bank jobs or mega heists yet, but it's only a matter of time before her daring or her loyalty will be tested. If she kills or hurts someone then I'll never get her back. She has a warped sense of loyalty to her friends. She'll protect people she cares about like a bloody lioness defends her cubs. I'm not her friend, I'm just her boring brother."

"Does she know you're a..."

"Spy? Of course not. 'Hey sis, you can't hang around crims and thieves and killers because you don't have her majesty's permission to do so, but I can'. How do you think that would go down?"

"That's why you're taking all the scrappy little assignments that Pond's dishing out." I struggle to sit upright. "He's paying you in information by tracking Domino."

"He's not tracking Domino. Oh he knows what I'm doing and I'm sure he has a file on his desk from some poor intelligence analyst on the Middle East desk. What he does do is give me time on our computer net. It helps *me* keep track of her. And I've haven't had to intervene yet." His voice drifts and for a while I think he's gone to sleep, then, "Even if I do go in and scoop her up, what then? She's proven to all of us that nine to five isn't for her."

"Do you know where she is now?"

"Dubai, the last time I went into the system. I found her location and a report of a suicide from the top of the Burj Al Arab. A woman matching Domino's description. I had to call in a private favour from the head of the Middle East station to establish that it wasn't her."

"Jesus hen, why didn't you say something?"

"I didn't want to bother you with a family matter."

This is the Pond side of him, the cold analytical and ruthless part, which is like a lit fuse to my anger. "Don't give me that blood is thicker than water bollocks! Look what my family brings; a mother I've never met, a back-stabbing brother, kidnappings, hostile takeovers and a father desperately trying to regrow neurons which may never fire properly again."

It's nearly five in the morning according to the glowing hands on the alarm clock on his side of the bed. I slap my feet flat on the floor and pull on the tracksuit from yesterday. Before I go out of the bedroom I say, "You can choose your friends but you can't choose your family."

We've had fights before but they were wars of words. He's never raised a hand to me. Sometimes one of us leaves the scene so that we don't allow verbal anger to transmute into something more active.

I kicked off my shoes when we arrived last night and they are still on the floor by the door. I want to just run away but it's not easy to do that in ballet flats. Pacing around down stairs I come across a cupboard full of trainers and wellies.

Jo's favourite café doesn't open until at least 6, just in time to catch the early morning commuters. I brew myself a quick cuppa, and, while the kettle boils, try on a few of the running shoes. A paint splattered pair seem to fit the best. Seb doesn't come down; probably figuring that having lit the fuse he should stay away from the initial explosion. I add a lot of milk to the tea and drink it in long gulps, then I lace up the trainers. As I leave, I drop the deadbolt behind me so that the door won't be left unlocked; not the best for a secure safe house. I don't take any keys, just my phone and my wallet. The cold hits me the minute I walk out of the door. I can't go back now, I'm locked out. So onwards I go into the chilly morning. The pavement feels solid under my feet. I walk past the house next door, which has a 'To Let' sign in the garden. Then I jog. On the grass of Wandsworth Common, I let loose, sprinting across the open ground, eyes open and alert for any suspicious looking dark patches that could be dog poo.

I pass an older guy sitting on a bench, his shaggy old English sheepdog straining at his leash to reach the pond. The old guy sips from a paper cup. I recognize the logo, 'Café Nervosa'. Must open earlier than I thought. Good job too, I've run myself ragged.

I point myself in the general direction of Wands-worth Common High Street. Soon I'm standing in a queue that has about the same ratio of briefcases to tracksuits. The radio is on, tuned to one of the local stations.

"Evacuations continue for central London where work-men unearthed what a statement described as a UXD or 'Unexploded Device' in the foundations of the soon to be built and highly touted 'Bressenden Plaza' development."

A groan goes up around me.

"Buckingham Palace is not affected, a bit of good news. Although Victoria Station and some Underground stations have been closed. The underground network is, presently, not affected."

I take a window seat, and sip my coffee, wrestling a question which has been bothering me since we got kicked out yesterday.

Maccallans is like one of those gyroscopes that you can play with. Set it spinning and for a while everything will be stable, as it starts to lose momen-tum the gyroscope rapidly loses stability and in the end plummets to the ground or just plain keels over. It could be days, even weeks, before we can get back to HQ. It's not the big things that worry me, it's the accumulation of small things that if not nipped in the bud can wreak havoc.

Several hours later,

"The rent is £1710,00 pcm."

"I only need it for two or three days," I protest. We're standing in the house next door to Bernie's safe house. We, is me and an estate agent who is treating me like a fish with a hook in its mouth. He names a per diem price of five hundred and fifty quid and pronounces it his 'final offer'. Okay, I didn't tell him that I'm the CEO and we could afford what he's askin', but a) right now my scots' streak is a mile wide, and b) there's nothing wrong wit ma mental maths. I'm no wasting the company's money. If he'd just said a thousand quid for the week I would've taken it and we could be here longer than a week, much longer.

"Okay, you talked me into it," I say. "I'll take it for the month. How soon can you draw up the paperwork?"

He gapes.

"Er."

"Good, that's settled. Oh and I want to move in today."

"I, er, I'm not able to authorize..."

"Take you a couple of hours to whip up some papers for me to sign, I understand. Would you prefer cash or bankers draft?" I answer my own question. "Banker's draft of course. Best be above board with all this. I'll be back here with someone from legal and you can hand over the keys." He mechanically sticks his hand into the top pocket of his Burton's special and hands over a business card.

I watch the poor sod drive off. Yes I steamrollered him and yes he deserved it. I didn't push as hard as I could've though. I want this place, the dining room alone is long enough to work as an office.

Bernie appears from next door, sipping from a steaming mug of tea.

"Seb's gone to make his report. He said to tell you he's sorry about earlier and you'd understand. He'll make it up to you. He didn't say anything about you buying the house next door."

I sum up what I've been up to.

"Who knows how long we'll be locked out. Now I just have to summon the shadow board."

"I've heard of a shadow cabinet but shadow board that's a new one on me."

I'm mortified I've even said it out loud.

"Oh come on, young lady, I'm a sad old pensioner with no friends. Who am I going to tell? And when it comes to private stuff, I am a vault."

"Let me call my legal people first or the man at Burton's is going to be back here with the paperwork before the ink on my banker's draft is dry."

CHAPTER 10

"We've got green or PG," Bernie calls from the kitchen where he's rummaging through a cupboard. "Or some very ancient Earl Grey."

"Green please." I pull up my contact for the legal department, Ted Gorey. He answers and we have a brief chat whilst his wife cadges a pen and some paper from the nearest Waitrose employee (seems I've caught him in the middle of the weekly shop.) Gorey's pretty no nonsense. He promises to obtain a banker's draft, and the attending documents and have them here in the next hour. Then he passes me over to his wife who writes down the address using Gorey's back as her blotter. "I'm wearing my down parka," she says. "If the pen goes through the fabric

I'll be hemorrhaging feathers up and down the aisles."

"And we wouldn't want that." I say, signing off and making another call to the head of the IT department.

A mug lands next to my elbow. I end that call and sip without looking. Ugh! Milk in green tea, and stewed green tea at that!

Bernie, in another violently floral shirt, takes the chair next to me.

"Shadow board, do tell."

"The actual board won't let me do anything. If I put up a proposal it gets shot down faster than a clay pigeon. I can't bulldoze the old codgers, Sorry Bernie, no offence."

"None taken."

"I found an ally, our new'ish head of HR, Philly Forrester."

Summing up our first meeting and plenty of subsequent ones, along with the fact that Seb dug deep into her background. I get to the meat.

"So let me guess she recruited the heads of department."

"Ooch no, hen. We brought in their deputies, but not all of them."

"She vetted them, then Seb *vetted* them. Once a month our shadow board meets and we work on influencing the heads of department to either make changes or put proposals forward to the board. We sacrifice a few, which means I support them and they get voted down."

"Doesn't the board shoot down your new hires?"

"Nae, there's a loophole which enables Philly to hire and fire below management level independently. No board interference."

"Remind me never to play chess with you."

"I don't play chess."

Bernie, whose ears are clearly sharper than mine gets up and vanishes into the hall.

"Your polyester prince estate agent has returned, also a van full of, wow that is ballsy, you recruited the entire IT department onto your shadow board?"

"Of course not! D'ya think we're mental, hen?

"We can't do business without access to computers, but Seb background checked all our IT personnel and he found no end of bad habits and mad hacking skills, one of them even hacked the bank account of an actual Nigerian prince. They don't have any prison time between them but they'd blackmail their own grannies if they thought it would get them anywhere. I called them because we need them, not because they're shadow board. Time to go and be the boss. I'll call back 'thanks for the tea' so it looks like you were being neighbourly. Oh and try not to let them see you."

"I'll be quiet as the proverbial church mouse."

The estate agent left with the banker's draft and my signature. I'm armed with a copy of the month's lease and a photocopy of the draft (You can't be too careful).

IT department came through good. They are _so_ getting an extra bonus. With a single purchase order number, they sourced most of the materials they needed to set up a network from the local Maplins. They moved like a colony of ants, cabling, setting up Wi-Fi routers, and putting a bunch of terminals and printers in. They linked us into the Wi-Fi at our offices, which is still happily running away in the background because it never gets turned off.

A call on the company wide intranet brings a motley group to my rented door.

I set up a conference call with the head offices; again, because of automation the regular orders are being filled and shipped from our warehouses. The bills are still going out; the money is still coming in. It is pleasing to see that the systems once put into place can run with just a wee tweak of human interference.

My two main concerns are new business and enquiries about stocking our brand for big events. Those come in through Jo's email which she hasn't been able to access as we don't have a work-from-home program, and even if she could log in, her dial-up modem would take hours to download and process all the emails she gets in a day.

I am surprised and humbled by the people who do turn up: all the shadow board members — Jo, Philly, Jeannine, the mercurial deputy head of security, Selima, Philly's second, Alex, our most recent PR hire, along with Roger something or other from sales, Peter, from accounting, Tania one of our receptionists and a couple of others.

"Look at us," Alex comments, looking around the room. "Are we here to overthrow the old guard?" He says it with enough levity that it passes as a joke. He takes a stack of PR related printouts from Jo and I watch him go to a desk at the far end of the long dining room.

Alex Mathis was my first, actually my only, hire. In the few days after the announcement, the press conferences and the interviews, I carved out the time to do a couple of things: promote the assistant director of communications to head of internet security, and cement our offer to Alex to be our online content director. His file included a personal letter he wrote to Garrett when he was still at University and his qualifications were impeccable. When I hired him he was languishing at an 'artsy-fartsy' (his words) advertising agency, 'spit balling' ideas at his boss who was two years behind him at Uni. In twenty-six year old Alex's eyes that made him an 'effin teenager'. Garrett had interviewed Alex and noted himself as 'very impressed with the lad'. Then the whole Fergus takeover craziness happened. When the dust cleared, I brought Alex in.

While he has revamped our online presence and insisted that we get on board with the plethora of new social media platforms, there's one problem. Alex wanted to work with Garrett, not me–and he never fails to remind me of that fact. He doesn't loathe me but he doesn't like me either. I can handle that.

Selima takes the personnel issues. Jeannine and Peter go out and return with a filter coffee maker, a dozen or so mugs, plates, cups, and a cool box containing ground coffee, milk, and bottled water nesting in ice. I notice Peter taking a picture of the receipt with his phone, then going to a terminal and starting to do accounting things. Tania works with Jo on correspondence. I stand there and marvel at how well they work together.

So well in fact that there's nothing for *me* to do. Oh wait, I can make them all coffee. I go into the kitchen, set out the cups, and plug in the coffee machine. Jeanine comes in as I'm pouring water in.

"Jo told me about the café on the high street. I've called in an order for us: sandwiches and pastries. I'm on my way now to get it."

"Use this." I toss her my credit card. "Don't worry about getting a receipt."

"I'll try and get an emergency sign while I'm out. I need to establish some evacuation routes. The garden is big, hemmed in by fences. And no fire doors."

I take the coffee carafe out and go round handing out mugs, and milk and sugar. "Pastries and sandwiches are on the way."

"Jeanine mentioned something about getting signage," Peter pipes up from his makeshift desk. "I hope she keeps a note of her expenses."

"I'm sure she will." I pour for him. "Milk?"

I take my tea and wander down the garden, having gingered up the staff, as da would put it, I think I deserve a short break.

"How goes it over there?" Bernie's question comes from the other side of the fence.

I explain what's going on, and about the emergency procedures that Jeanine wants to set up.

"Thinking with his health and safety hat on isn't he?"

"*She* is. And she could bring down health and safety on us like a ton of bricks."

"Ah those killers of fun since 1976."

"Mary!" Jo's standing out on the concrete patio. "I've got Nicolas Castro on the phone asking for you."

Castro heads up our Spanish operation. He was one of the people I couldn't get hold of on our earlier conference call.

"Nico, cómo estás?" I speak Spanish but Nico usually wants to chat in English. He's very proud of his command of the language, even though he does get bogged down with slang. This way he gets to choose.

"Good, good. I see I missed a call from you. There's no need to explain; our guest said it was all a bit spur of the moment."

"Your guest? Sorry Nico you've lost me."

"Harrington-Smythe?"

Typical, I think. The only one of the MAC who would think of wrangling a freebie during a crisis.

"It's my own fault," Nico continues. "I offered him a tour of our estate the last time we visited London."

"He's staying *with* you?"

"Well, I couldn't just park him in a hotel could I?"

Yes, I think, *Yes you could.*

"Well, keep him away from the sauce."

"I will?" Nico's tone turns quizzical. "Any news on when the London office will reopen?"

"It's already open. That's what I was calling to tell you. We've set up a temporary HQ in the wilds of Wandsworth."

"Wandsworth." I hear him stab a couple of buttons. "That's not even on this google map."

"I wanted to be as far away from the blast zone as possible. They've already extended it once."

"Are you reconvening the board?"

"Nae, Nico, there's no need. I'm handling this maself. We've got a skeleton staff. Most of them are the IT boys and girls."

"Computers, hey." I think he means 'eh', but he's still talking. Something about 'impressing my father'.

My da doesn't know yet. He was the other person we couldn't reach earlier.

"Talk to you soon Nico. Love to Venitzia and Ava."
***

It might have taken six hours but I'm fairly confident that we have the office back under control. The head of IT set me up with Skype before he left for the day.

The last thing I did before calling Garrett was to phone Daz and invite him out to our Wandsworth branch as Jo has dubbed it. Sometimes you have to blow your own trumpet. We know we're back. Soon the rest of the business grapevine will know too.

Deep breath in. Time to Skype da.

Two hours later.

I need to end this trial by Skype. How I miss the days of being able to cut someone off by 'going into a tunnel'. A hand appears on the screen.

"Come along Mr. Maccallan," da's starched Swiss nurse has him by the upper arm. "Neurons need nutrients."

I'm saved. "Bye da."

A sharp rap at the front door. Seb looks how I feel, wrung out, even a little bit shaken, except I'm pretty sure I don't have a grubby face.

"Come in, hen."

"All this in a day?" His lips purse in a silent whistle. "They could use you in logistics."

"My da wouldn't agree with you. I just had to defend 'wasting company money' and 'knee jerk reactions'. His parting shot was, 'on your head be it'.

"You think you've made a mistake?"

"Nae, hen."

I can see him start to relax for a brief second before his expression goes from shaken to stricken.

"What's the matter? You look like da the day he dropped Fergus' ashes and we had to vac him up."

"There's been a..." he verbally stumbles over the word, "de.. development."

"You found the train?"

"No, we found the driver."

"Not following you, hen. You lost Coltrane's body?"

"I didn't lose anything!" Seb snaps. Then he calms and rubs at his face. "Sorry, Mary. I'm in a bit of a pickle."

Typical British understatement. With an employee I'd tell them to 'spit it out'. I swallow my impatience. "On a scale of one to ten how bad is it?"

"Seven to ten," again with the face rub. "Coroner wasn't one of our usuals. He went on the ID and the physical characteristics before he fell prey to motion sickness."

There's a tempting hook there. Daz thought mobile morgue, it seems he was right.

"He did take some blood and the tests came back this morning. Coltrane was blood type O, the blood taken from the body was AB negative. That got our regular coroner, back from his holidays, interested. He ran the tests again and this is who we have in the morgue." The folder he's been cradling slaps onto the desk.

"Lars Thorsen?"

"Norwegian national, house mate to Patrick Coltrane. He was still living at their shared address when I apprehended him this morning, Mary. He's the one who tried to mug your friend Daz."

"Coltrane?"

"No! Thorsen. When they handed me the folder, I had to hide the fact I knew who he was or that would've led to some *very* awkward questions. "Don't look at me like that, how was I to know the two were connected."

I should tell him about Daz now, but he's already talking again.

"We've been questioning Coltrane all day. He cracked like an egg when we put him into interrogation but then Pond turned up with Higgins in tow and had me kicked out. So I went back to looking for the train. Later, outside Paddington Green police station, Higgins slipped me a recording of their interrogation. He told me that we should invest in the shit creek paddle company because that's where Coltrane left them. So it sounds like he wasn't as forth coming with Pond as he was starting to be with me."

"Speaking of being forth coming, something I should tell you about Daz."

"Can it wait a bit. I'm running on hamster shavings and caffeine fumes. Bernie's ordered fish and chips."

Seb calls cereal bars hamster shavings because he says that's what they taste like. He wraps an arm around my waist and waits whilst I lock the office.

"I never asked how the first day went?"

"It went well." We walk down the path. "I've actually made more impactful decisions today than in most of my CEOship. I didn't tell da, but having people co-operate with me without giving me side-eye or throwing out blocks did that." I sweep my hand back towards the house. "The shadow board came, of course, and the entire IT department. I couldn't have done it without them, no matter what your opinion of them is."

"All I said was that they are easily corruptible."

I don't want to get into that argument again.

Next door Bernie has procured fish and chips, (mushy peas optional). After we've eaten and Seb has removed the ash from his face he takes a DVD out of his inside suit pocket and vanishes upstairs with his laptop.

He comes back down a bit later.

"I need a second opinion. I'm missing something, just not sure what."

He puts the DVD into the player underneath the TV in the dining room.

"This is the interview conducted with Coltrane. He didn't clam up like I expected after I left. In fact he was singing like Charlotte Church at a benefit concert. His words, as you'll both see, are incredibly troubling."

Pond and Higgins are doing the questioning. The camera is on Coltrane. He looks ordinary, a little pasty. A flat cap he was wearing when Seb arrested him now lays on the table in front of him, brim pointed at his inquisitors like a stuck out tongue. He doesn't look rattled. In fact, he appears to be enjoying himself.

"Let's start with the night you took the train."

"Oh I didn't. That was my roommate, Lars. It was his plan." There's a sound of someone scribbling something down, then Higgins speaks again.

"Thorsen's is the body we recovered?"

"Yes. After he'd 'borrowed' the train and we'd hitched up the carriage he'd been moving around, he said we needed a body to set the plan in motion and he went off to get one. I waited ages. Then he comes charging back into the tunnel, off balance, yelling something about ninjas. He slipped and 'bbzzztt', the murderous third rail."

"Leaving you to carry out the rest of his plan."

"No." Coltrane's expression is smug.

"What do you mean, no?" Pond interrupts, "He told you his plan. He must have."

Coltrane shakes his head, defiance in his eyes. "He didn't tell me his plan. He told me his objective and asked for my help."

"You never asked how he was going to achieve his objective?"

"Why should I? Lars knew what he was doing, clever he was."

"Not that clever," Higgins points out, his tone dry. "He is dead after all."

"Yeah, but he needed a body to set the plan in motion. A body was provided." Coltrane sounds strangely pleased with himself.

Watching him, I feel a shudder rising up my spine. *Thorsen wasn't trying to mug Daz, he was procuring a body.* The interrogation continues and I have to mentally spool back through the words to catch up.

"He said you lot would turn up and question us, and look, here you are. Heavy mob too, just like he said. What took you so long?"

"What was his objective?" This from Pond.

"To finish what Guy Fawkes started. Those are his exact words."

"Lock him back up."

"Don't I get a phone call?" Coltrane says as two hands grab hold of him and lift him out of frame. "Nah, just kidding. Who would I call?" The screen goes blank.

CHAPTER 11

"Bloody hell," Bernie mutters under his breath.

"Your friend Daz doesn't know how lucky he is," Seb looks at me.

"About that, about Daz; something you should know, hen."

"What?"

"Promise me you won't fly off the handle."

I tell him about Daz, the newsroom tip, our out of hour's station visit, and the body that he followed out to Docklands.

"He overheard your boys while they were waiting for you. He knows about the train." Before Seb can open his mouth I rush on. "And he can help. His great—great—grandpa, Patil, helped to map the first underground rail network. He talked about ghost stations and ghost lines and then the bomb disposal team arrived and we got separated. He's coming out here tomorrow. I'm giving the Independent's business page an exclusive."

"We took a bike, his bike, how did he...?" Seb glares at me. "You weren't stuck in traffic when you called me. You were already in Docklands."

"Daz was in over his head," I say, not backing down. "He just didn't know it."

"Am I on the list?"

"List?"

"Of people you'd drive across London to save."

"Top of it."

"I should bloody well think so." His voice is still semi-angry but I catch the ghost of a smile.

"Offer him an exclusive in exchange for the maps."

"He's a journalist. What makes you think he'll keep his word?"

"I know him and I trust both of you."

"Pond will do his nut if he finds out."

"I'm nae going to tell him. Are you?"

Seb's phone purrs on the chair beside him.

"Yes?" He listens. "Good work."

"They searched the house. Thorsen had maps of London. Several massive architectural blue prints tacked to the walls of his room and on the floor. Enough C4 to reduce the house and most of that row to rubble."

Bernie looks at Seb and me. "With C4 in the mix, I think we both know what that means. We have to find that train. And if you can get the okay from Pond, I think I can lay hands on a way to cover our search area quicker."

"Speak of the devil." A large limousine pulls up outside the safe house. "I shouldn't be surprised that my team shared information with Pond."

Seb gets up to go outside. Bernie stops him.

"Let him come to you."

Bernie opens the door. He doesn't say 'come in', just tramps back toward the kitchen. A few moments later Pond enters the living room, taking off his coat and folding it over the only empty chair, which Seb dragged over so that whoever sits in it will have their back to the door. Not one word has been exchanged. If Seb is content to keep silent then so am I. Bernie, returning from the kitchen, bangs a tray of filled coffee cups down onto the table with all the grace of a grumpy bear, and withdraws. His heavier than usual footsteps pause halfway up the wooden staircase. Pond's eyes dart a micro-second glance in that direction. He probably doesn't even realize he did it. In the plan Seb hastily stitched together while the Director of MI6 walked up the path; Bernie being out of sight, but close by, will mess with Pond's head.

Seb says his lines, he's precise. He lays out the possible threat and his plan of action, then waits to see if Pond augments his ideas or shoots him down.

"A dead man may have planted a bomb somewhere in the city, underground, and it may have been there for some time. Am I missing anything?"

"When you put it like that..." I butt in.

"That's exactly right, sir," Seb agrees. This side of him, the one that sides with Pond, annoys the knackers off me. "Bernie tells me he has access to some equipment we can use to cover a lot of ground in a short time."

Pond shudders at Bernie's name.

"Next week it will be November, a most difficult month."

Seb quietly agrees.

Pond turns to me. "Maccallan, do you know how many times since I've been director some misguided idiot has tried to blow up the houses of parliament on the 5th of November?"

"More than once?"

"*Twenty one times*, Maccallan. We've thwarted them each time, and some of our thwarting has been pure luck. Most of them try and do it with actual gunpowder, symbolism being sooooo important these days. But *any* explosive compound from black powder to C4 to sticks of ACME bloody dynamite bought in the run up to November 5th gets a visit from," whatever he said was supplanted in my brain by 'the goon squad'.

"Something funny, Maccallan?"

"Nae, just nerves. It's not every day that you find out that the ground beneath your feet might be riddled with explosives."

"And we can't just focus on parliament. The device could be anywhere in central London, and we don't even know how big it is," Seb throws in.

"Parliament is the most likely target, Miller. You've done your job. I'm..." Pond's tongue can't quite wrap around the word 'grateful'. "...Gra hmm ful for your efforts. Consider yourself stood down."

"No. I want my job back." Seb doesn't stumble over his words like Pond did.

"Miller you were declared unfit. I..."

Seb leans across the table and for a brief moment I think he's about to grab the director by the lapels. "If I'm so bloody unfit for duty, why keep me around, feed me scraps, let me off the leash when you need me. I work for her majesty's government, not for you."

"You'd be working as a security guard at Tescos or a nightclub bouncer if I hadn't kept you sharp." Pond retorts.

"So *use* me! I want to stop this and deal with the people responsible. If you don't..." he leaves the rest of his threat hanging between them.

Pond's eyes glitter, there is no other way to describe it.

"My people will take over the main investigation. We still answer to the HMG you hold so dear, and as such we have to follow protocol. We will focus on parliament because it *is* the obvious target. You can pursue your more unorthodox enquiries. If you haven't put a stop to this by the morning of November

5th, I will have no choice but to issue an evacuation order for the Houses of Parliament. On top of the present from the 1940's, all of central London will be shut down. And I will issue the order based on information provided by you. The media will have a field day, and I will dangle the corpse of your career from the flagpole at Vauxhall Cross as a warning to those who come after you."

"And when I *do* stop this." Seb's face is inches away from Pond's. "I get my job back, my team back, and full pension and back pay."

"I've given you my deadline, Miller. I can't give you any more resources than Bernard and Maccallan. If Bernard's contacts turn up anything, you can pursue those angles until they're exhausted."

"Sir, for Bernie's idea to work I'll need free access to the blast zone for myself and my team."

"Starting when?"

"The earliest we can go in is tomorrow night."

"Very well."

Seb's lack of a 'thank you, sir' is noted by both Pond and myself.

"And you'd better hope that nothing blows up in the meantime because if it does, even if it's those bloody WWII bombs, I'm going to blame you."

He gets up and walks out, leaving his half full coffee cup on the table. I can't help thinking that if this was a movie, this would be M goading her agent, knowing that his dogged determination would save the day. In real life, Pond is just being his uptight asshole of a self. His limousine glides away into the dusk.

CHAPTER 12

I was chasing sleep last night and never quite catching up to it. This has left me cranky, badly in need of coffee and catapulted into a crisis which I really didn't need first thing of any morning.

Jo comes over to my desk. "I've got Senor Castro," she says.

"Put him on speaker would you?"

"I don't think that's a good idea, Mary."

"Nico," is all I get the chance to say before a stream of molten Spanish melts my eardrums.

"Whoa, hold on," I say, in Spanish. "He did, what? Nico, I told you to keep him away from the port. Sauce *is* alcohol. No. Slow down. I know you're angry. I would be too in your place. I'm angry *for* you. What have you done with him? Is he still in Spain?"

I've drawn a curious crowd, which is what this PR catastrophuck is going to do, draw a feeding frenzy of paparazzi.

At first blush it doesn't sound so bad, Harrington-Smythe got so bladdered last night that he pissed in Castro's swimming pool. Unfortunately at the time the pool contained Castro's film star wife and their two year old daughter Ava. The old fart exposed himself to both of them and turned the water purple.

Castro grinds out that he's kicked H-S off his estate and has been stewing on the matter until he could unload (pardon the pun) on me.

I make all the soothing noises I can because Nico is a tricky character. He's very hospitable and, handled correctly a pussy cat (my da is godfather to little Ava). H-S's golden shower however has awakened a full-on fire breathing dragon beastie.

Later that day:

When I first got Castro on Skype, I let him rant and rave to get a lot of the vitriol out of his system. Now I've just issued a memo to the board that all their company travel is suspended 'Effective Immediately'. It's one of the many things I promised Castro, to get him to calm down.

He started making demands after that. I let him push me a little way. For instance, he wants H-S kicked out of the company. H-S is in Castro's words "A maldito, elephant blanco, he's so old he pees in Morse code. And he *laughed* when Venitizia began to scream at him to stop."

After that there was a litany of ways H-S had abused his hospitality. I focused on thinking calm thoughts and looking straight into Castro's brown eyes. Truth be told I'm not Skype's biggest fan. On the phone I can yawn and even focus on the beautiful landscape painting on the wall above the visitor's sofa in my office. I did think about putting makeup on, but thought that the barefaced look would work better with the urgency of the situation. The word yawn entered my head and now I want to.

Slicing through his sentences. I agreed to remove H-S.

"The simplest way is to feed him to the press. Your press chaps are part flesh eaters."

Castro breaks into a wide grin. I immediately wipe it from his face.

"The problem with that Nico, is that bullshit spreads, and some of it will stick to ye no matter how hard you try and keep it away. I mean look at you, handsome successful, head honcho of the company, Hollywood wife; you're a gift to the gossip columns. They'd be milking you for weeks."

He preens and then sinks like a ruined soufflé at the thought of all those gringos laying siege to his estate.

"Is there another way?"

See, this is one of the best things da ever taught me, the subtle art of manipulation. Make the other party think it was their idea. As soon as Castro asked that question, I knew I'd got him.

"I could threaten to throw him into journalist infested waters if he doesn't resign."

"No parachute?"

"He'll get an engraved watch and a few shares. They didn't do parachutes in my da's day."

Castro asked for some time to think. "Maybe now isn't the time to pressure him." I manufacture a yawn.

"And of course, Nico, it'll give me a chance to find out if we've located the wee idiot."

He winces at my use of the word 'wee', which I knew was a mistake as soon as it came out of my mouth.

"Here's my private mobile number, Nico. You have a pen?" I wait while he gets one, then reel off the number. "Call me when you've come to a decision as to how we handle this." We, the inclusive, as in we're all in this together.

Jo comes up to my desk holding, bless her, a tray with a pot of green tea, a can of Red Bull and a wrap from the Thai takeaway on the high street.

"I've got Garrett holding on line one."

"Tell him I'll call him back in five."

In the end it's ten. You cannot rush a Thai chicken wrap with peanut satay. If you do you are more likely to be wearing it than eating it.

"Any sign of H-S?" I ask Jo,

"Nothing yet."

I Skype Garrett, in order to keep my personal line free for Castro.

The cheerful sounds of Skype connecting are at odds with the gravity I feel right now. Garrett Maccallan appears on the screen, a snow covered alp behind his left shoulder. Never mind re-growing brain cells, the Swiss air seems to have stopped the aging process. If anything he looks more clear eyed than the last time we spoke. But there is no glint in his eye, and his mouth is set in a frown.

"Da, how are you?"

"Not a social call, lassie. What the hell have you done now?"

"Oh god, which board member came whining to you?"

"Harrington-Smythe."

"You've heard from H-S?" the little me on the screen's eyebrows raise in surprise. "Where is he?"

"He's in Spain, and in a right state. Says something about you having him kicked off Nicolas Castro's estate."

I waste no time in setting da straight.

Once I've summed up he gives me that exasperated fatherly look that means, again I've gone too far.

"Do not give me that look. The board are not touching this with a barge pole. They dropped this turd in my lap and I'm dealing with it. Castro is at this moment mulling over whether to feed H-S to the press. You know what will happen if we screw up this partnership. He'll give his considerable resources to our competitor and we'll lose a massive slice of Latin American business to boot. We need his influence over there."

"Hmmm,"

The mention of business and da's favourite subject, profits, gives him pause.

"Did H-S give you a number?" I ask. "I need to speak to him. I'm pretty sure he knows just how much trouble he is in right now. What he doesn't know is that he has options."

"Let me call him. It will be better coming from me."

I could argue that I'm CEO not him, but it would come across as whinging, and it saves me from having to talk to the wee idiot and possibly lose my temper.

I lay out both options. "Tell him if I don't hear from him by the end of business today, I will feed him to the Spanish press, and I will make sure that they have all the juicy details, including *who* he peed on."

"You're bluffing right, lassie?"

"Da, on the Ratner scale of PR disasters this is a 9.9. I am nae bluffing."

"I'll be in touch." He cuts the connection and I'm left staring at an empty screen.

***

My interview with Daz is looming, and radio silence from both Castro and da.

For something to do, and to keep my mind off the imagined sentence *'Loch-Maccallan's share price nosedived today on the news of an indiscretion by a board member'*. I go onto the internet and search Guy Fawkes. Of the twenty-one attempts to blow up Parliament there are zero mentions.

Thomas Harrington-Smythe is alleged to have urinated into a swimming pool where movie actress, Venititia Castro, and two year old daughter Ava were relaxing.

Castro and her daughter were sprayed by Harrington-Smythe. Both were admitted to a local hospital where they are currently under observation.

Both my mobile and Skype start off at the same time. I reject the Skype call. Da can wait.

"Senor Castro, thanks for calling me back."

"My apologies for taking so long. I had to consult with Tia. She has convinced me that it would be better for both sides if this matter could be dealt with in private. She requires certain conditions to be met, which we have already discussed. She also wants him to donate a portion of his salary to a local children's charity here in Barcelona."

"I'm sure that can be arranged." I switch gears for a moment. "How are Tia and Ava doing?"

"They are okay. I had the company doctor come out and check on them."

"Tell Tia I owe both of them a shopping spree next time she is in London. Ava still likes those Ice cream drinks (I nearly said floats but managed to substitute in time) in Hamleys?"

"She does, and I will let my ladies know." Over the air I hear Castro's voice become more businesslike.

"Have you spoken with him yet?"

I can't help a tiny pause. "Not yet. We are still trying to locate him. I have a third party attempting contact."

Castro sees straight through that. "I hope your father can make him see sense. Call me as soon as you have something. Remember, Mary, option 2 is still on the table."

"We'll talk soon Nico."

I check the time. Daz is late which is most unlike him. I'll give him ten minutes to allow for traffic and then I'll call.

I'm out in the kitchen grabbing myself a coffee when a taxi pulls up. Daz gets out and stands on the pavement. The driver winds down the window, yells something and hands Daz some change, then pulls away.

Daz stays where he is. As I get closer I can see the dazed expression on his face. His body is here, but his mind...?

"Daz?" I touch his arm, and as I do I see his phone clenched in the other hand.

He turns towards the sound of my voice, eyes unseeing.

"Hey!" This time I used a bit more force and he seems to focus on me. I get the feeling that another slight tap might send him into a million shards.

"Come inside," I say, leading him by the arm. Abandoning the idea of sitting him next to my desk in front of the curious eyes of the staff, instead I lead him through their midst and out onto the patio where, after I've closed the sliding door, we cannot be overheard. Out here there's a fire pit, a sad looking picnic table, and a couple of patio chairs which are supposed to be comfy if you like your chairs covered in plastic. I sit him down and take the seat across from him, my wrists resting lightly on the flimsy table.

"What's the matter, hen?"

I have seen Daz excited, elated, scared, wounded but never like this. You rarely see men allow themselves to go to pieces. They don't cry in public. In my experience they rarely cry in private.

Daz dissolves before my eyes, no other word for it. The assured and astute man mutates into a little boy. Tears and snot mingle on his face. His almond bloodshot eyes framed by those spider leg lashes and heavy brows that he swears he never plucks.

I try and draw lines in my life. With Seb and me, the line was erased long ago. With Daz, the professional and personal have started to blur. For instance, I'd never drive clear across town in rush hour to rescue a member of the board from MI6, but I'd do it for Seb, for Jo, for Garrett (of course), and for Charlie; and Daz because I did just that only a few days ago. He removes a giant cloth hankie from his pocket and continues to produce his weight in waterworks.

Never, never in my life have I been called maternal; the urge to have kids has never kicked in with me. So it's a surprise to both of us when I stand and pull him up into a hug. "C'mere, hen."

For the briefest of seconds, I wonder if this is my mother's side. It sure as hell isn't Garrett's. I've only seen him cry a couple of times and his hugs are perfunctory, not because he doesn't love me, but because his emotions are zipped up tighter than a Scotsman's sporran.

Daz lets me pull him up. It would be bloody awkward to lean down and hug him while he's sitting in a plastic swathed chair. His tears, hopefully those are tears and not boogers, while still flowing, cease being as noisy. I hold him until he stops shaking. It feels like hours. Lime coriander and a pungent dose of sweat transfers from his shirt to my shoulder.

"What's happened, hen?"

He sinks back into the chair with some unpleasant sound effects, and I put some distance between us so that we can both get back a little of our dignity. I go back to the door, where Jo is hovering, and ask her for a couple of clean glasses and some airline miniatures (she brought in a supply yesterday which lives in her office drawer along with a case of red bull). She comes out and lays them on the table. We crack them, and while I pour half of mine into the glass, Daz chugs his.

"In your own time."

I don't want to push him, although all kinds of scenarios are playing out in my head. He got demoted, lost his job altogether, got kicked out of his leased apartment. There are several others, but I don't entertain any of those. Finally he speaks.

"My brother, Aayush. I talked to him on Skype like your friend suggested. He looked at my wound and told me I had done well, used my head, then berated me for getting into a situation where I almost got mugged. I made him promise not to tell my father."

He tears up again. More tissues, and the rest of my glass, which I push towards him, he downs without even wiping the rim clean.

"I got a phone call from my father on my way over here. My first thought was that Aayush had snitched on me and I cursed him for being a caring fool." His voice breaks on the word 'fool'. "Aayush is dead. He had a massive heart attack on base during an operation. He was gone before he hit the operating theatre floor."

"Oh Daz." My mother kicks in again, and again I'm out of the chair to comfort him.

"He was twenty-six," Daz says into my shirt. "Whole life ahead of him. He introduced me to Sunni, my wife to be."

"Jesus," I mutter, letting him slump back into the chair, and rushing back to the other side of the picnic table.

"Are you going home for the funeral?"

"I don't know, it won't be yet. They have to bring him home first and it will be a military funeral. I never agreed with him going into the military. I told him he could be a healer at home."

"You can have a private service as well as the military one," I say.

"My father will go all out. He will give Aayush the maximum honour the family can."

"At least you know both your parents," I counter, trying to bring the conversation back to a more even keel. "I was raised without a mother."

"Is she still alive?" I can see Daz's journalist curiosity sparking a fraction. I'd normally squash it, now I encourage it.

"No idea," I shrug. "I think about her sometimes. She could've kept me and not taken Garrett's money."

"I've never seen you like that before," Daz says. "I was expecting you to pep talk me, not mother me."

"I," hard to deny, "I wasn't, well I was, I haven't..." Flustered, I pull myself up short. "I think that might've been my ma's side coming out."

"Scottish?"

"Italian. I only know her first name."

"Your dad's never been married, has he?"

"Nae, he doesn't have the patience for a wife. He likes the thrill of the chase, wining, dining, wooing. Time and time again when I was growing up I'd meet his new lady friends. We'd get to know each other; brunches and shopping trips and holidays. I'd warm to them, or not, and as soon as da declared she was 'the one' for him they'd drift apart. He's not a lover he's an angler, catch and release."

Daz is paying much more attention now. A few years back I would've taken that as a red flag. Back when I didn't talk to journalists let alone trust one enough to let my guard down. I would've decided that he was faking, that his brother was still upright.

I have the board to thank for honing my skills. Kind words from a board member don't mean you walk away without a metaphorical knife between your shoulder blades.

"He raised you?"

"He had quite a bit of help," I concede. "He told me on more than one occasion that we kids were more interesting than adults, that we kept him young. If we bored him, his default setting was to pack us off to the movies. If he travelled we usually went with him. He used to joke that we were gold digger repellent."

"In my family we've had our fair share of those." Daz blows his nose. "Always westerners with no patience. As soon as those true colours fly, we're out. They even try chatting up my father. My mother is not amused."

A gentle tap on the glass behind us and Jo emerges carrying a pot of green tea and two cups.

"I thought you might need this," she says. Daz gathers his wits and smiles up at her.

"How very kind. Thank you Mrs. Jo."

He gets up. "I have taken up enough of your valuable time, Mary. Thank you for being the shoulder I needed." Jo withdraws. The door closes behind her. "Now I shall throw myself into my work and process the rest of my grief that way."

I try not to sound concerned. I fail. "Um, your missing train?"

"Yes, of course the missing train. My grandfather has been most helpful. Before my father's phone call I was making plans to visit one of the ghost stations tomorrow night. Those plans still stand."

I can't stop him going. Mebbe I can make him a better offer. "Could you put it off for a night?"

"Why ever would I do that?"

"I might have some contacts who are also looking for the train and your maps might help them."

"Why? I'd be sharing my exclusive," he shakes his head possibly at my stupidity at even suggesting such a thing, or maybe he's just saying 'no'.

"These people aren't journalists. Besides you're not thinking straight; not the best time to be rushing down into the bowels of the earth with just a torch and a map."

"I am not that deluded, Mary." Daz sniffs and rubs his eyes. "The guide my grandfather has contacted, Mr. Keyes..." Here I look down to try and hide my shock; *Fletcher Keyes?* "...he'll be with me the whole time."

"I'm sure Mr. Keyes would prefer to be fully pre-pared." My brain is winging it. Even I can hear that makes no sense. I don't even know the man.

"Well," Daz shuffles his feet, thinking. "I suppose.

"He wanted me to wait until the copies of the maps my grandfather is couriering to me had arrived."

"Come back here tonight, say 11 o'clock, and bring the maps. I'll introduce you to the team. You'll get your exclusive, I promise."

"Why so late?"

"Tube trains don't run after midnight."

"I'll come, but if I don't like what I see, I'll pass."

"Think you can walk through the open plan office with me again?"

"I think I can handle stares." We go back inside and everyone is suddenly very busy.

"Jo, could you order a taxi for Mr. Patel, prepaid, use my travel account."

"No, Mary, I can walk to the station." He looks around. "Where is the station from here?"

"Not happening, hen."

Once Daz has been seen safely into a taxi, I pick up the file sent by Nico before P-gate erupted, containing the new tax proposals the Spanish parliament is attempting to pass, and try to bore myself back to sanity. An hour later I call Seb.

CHAPTER 13

11 p.m:

Daz arrives carrying a canvas satchel. Seb and Bernie told me to stall him, so we have the interview that should've taken place this morning, which is very strange in a deserted office.

My phone rings.

"We're geared up and ready to go."

"Wait for me outside," I tell Daz. "I'm just going to lock up." CEO and security guard, what would da think of that?

I'm satisfied we're secure, and come out to find Daz pressed against the wall in the hall.

"What've you done?" he hisses. "They're here. How did they find me?"

Looking out at the road I can see why he's so concerned. A black panel van, hopefully not the same one we saw at Victoria with a dead body in it, sits idling at the kerb. Seb leans out of the back. "Are you two coming or would you prefer an invitation?"

Daz recognizes him instantly, his eyes bug.

Seb wheels Daz's bike down the ramp.

"Peace offering," he says. "It's fully serviced. My guys cleaned all the cylinders and it has a full tank of petrol."

He tosses Daz the keys, which he fumbles but doesn't drop.

"Follow us or we'll just meet you at Victoria. You brought the maps?"

"Of course."

"Slow down as you approach the road block on Vauxhall Bridge, that'll give them time to scan your license plate and wave you through. See you there, Daz."

I am not getting on the back of Daz's bike. (I never lean the right way. I nearly put my first boyfriend in a Glasgow ditch when I sat up in a corner and we ended up going straight on at a roundabout).

"We've got him," Seb says as soon as we pull away. Unable to help myself I sniffed when I got in——no eau de dead body. "At least I think we have."

Giving Daz the option to travel to Victoria under his own steam, and seeing me with Seb, knowing our connection, his curiosity must be piqued right now. I know mine would be. That should keep his mind off his brother for the moment. I need him focused.

By the time we arrive, I've put on dark blue coveralls and a vest in nuclear orange with MAINTENANCE in reflective lettering across the back. This, I'm told, is purely a precaution in case anyone sees us.

When Daz arrives, Seb takes him inside the van and whatever he says to him causes Daz to go Caucasian. I'm presuming it had something to do with his attempted mugging being more of a human sacrifice. We troop around the side, now all dressed alike. With Seb lugging a large hold-all, we reach the side entrance just across the road from the passport office. Bernie opens the door. He has a railway employee with him. They lead the way across the empty concourse and down into the tunnels.

Bernie's role in all this still eludes me. I know he's retired from the spy game and Seb said he wasn't a techie, but you could've fooled me. After Seb dumps the bag down on the platform, Bernie drops to his knees and unzips it to reveal lots of little rotors and plastic pieces. With a calculated efficiency he puts the pieces together; his hands seem to work apart from his body. He's looking at Seb and talking with him while his hands clip, snap, and twist the thing together. It reminds me of my da when he's assembling his carbon fibre fishing rods. Daz's map is unrolled and Seb overlays it on the map they've been using.

"Just as we thought. There's a raft of unused lines around here. I told you we needed a better map."

Daz steps closer for a look at Bernie's handywork. "It's a drone," he says, reaching out to touch it——or he would have if Seb hadn't stuck out an arm to stop him. "I've never seen one like that before though. Do these things even work down here?"

Bernie shoots him a pitying look. "This the journalist?"

Daz tries to introduce himself and Bernie dismisses him with, "Later."

He and Seb pore over the maps whilst we take a walk up and down the platform.

"How did you get mixed up in all this?" Daz asks.

"Did Seb make you sign the OSA?"

"I refused."

"Then I can't tell ya, hen."

Daz hurrumps his annoyance.

"You're lucky he let you down here. He's trusting you not to spill what you've seen. He could've left you locked in the van."

Whilst Daz is considering this Seb beckons us over. Bernie is busy tapping commands into a keyboard.

"I've programmed the map you gave me into quadrants." He acknowledges Daz with a brief nod. "I'll search each quadrant. If we see something that looks interesting, I'll pause the program and investigate further."

"How does it work underground?" Daz asks.

"It uses radio signals and an internal guidance system."

"You lost me."

"That was my intention. You're distracting my calculations, son. There's an equation I have to work through in my head to make sure this thing doesn't crash."

"Sorry." Daz steps back allowing Bernie more room. We wait for him to talk again.

"All this equipment is military spec," says Bernie, finally breaking his silence. He carefully screws a small box with a large lens onto the bottom of the drone so that it hangs unimpeded.

"This is not your father's Go Pro," he says, as he gestures for Seb to pick up the drone. "This little beauty can switch over to night vision in the disused tunnels, now that we know where they are." To Seb, "Lift it over your head, high as you can."

"It weighs a bloody ton," Seb complains as he lifts it up.

"You're the one who forgot to ask for the launch frame," Bernie counters. Then he presses a series of buttons and we can't talk, only watch. Both Daz and I clap our hands over our ears. The noise in here with all the sound reflections pinging back and forth is deafening.

Seb has no such luxury. He stands, knees slightly bent, arms rock solid. I'm watching him, not Bernie. The drone begins to rise. Seb can't see what is going on, but once he feels the upward pull he lets go. I would've stepped out from under the whirling rotors in case the thing fell back to earth. Seb releases both sides simultaneously and stands perfectly still, whipped by the rotor washes. The drone rises higher and glides out over the tracks. Bernie makes a couple of adjustments and moves it off into the tunnel where it hovers in the drone equivalent of 'parked'. Then he signals us all to the far end of the platform.

Bernie takes out a control box with levers and knobs all over it and a large military looking laptop. The last two items out of the bag are some overalls and a pair of night vision goggles.

"You lot are my eyes and ears. If you see anything, hit the pause button. That will pause the program and I'll know there's something up ahead." He steps into the overalls and zips them up. The control box straps go across his back and down his shoulders leaving the box resting against his stomach. He puts on the heavy pack, tightens the straps around his waist, and cinches down the shoulder straps.

"Why risk it?" Daz asks. "You could do all that from here."

"Why don't you stick to journalism," Bernie suggests. "Down here, the radio signal only extends so far," he pats the equipment on his back, "and so does the battery. I'm just a walking boosted radio signal and retrieval asset. My only other job is to not step on the third rail. If you'll excuse me I have to rendezvous with my target."

"Oh," Daz says, crestfallen. "My apologies. Please let's find this thing."

I turn away from Bernie and say to Daz, "Don't worry, hen, I'm in the dumb—dumb club too. I had the same question only you beat me to it."

Bernie puts a headset over his ears, places the mic close to his lips, then dangles his legs over the edge of the platform. With the goggles pushed up to his forehead, he lowers himself onto the rails, keeping well to the left of the third one, he shuffles off into the tunnel.

"Comms check," Seb says into the radio.

Bernie raises a hand; "Check, check." He shuffles into the tunnel, only stopping to lower the NVGs into place.

"Who ya gonna call?" Daz sends a salute at Bernie's departing back.

"Ghostbusters," I say.

"What?" says Seb.

We gather around the laptop. Seb pulls the padded canvas bag in front of it and we sit in a semicircle, eyes locked onto the screen. Think brownies round a campfire.

The first quadrant is a bust. Nothing but grimy bulbless red and green lights, warning signs, plenty of graffiti on the walls, and a shed load of filthy tunnels. It is the weirdest sensation because Bernie has programmed the drone to hover at the same eye level you would get when sitting on a tube train. So weird not to have carriages surrounding you.

The drone doesn't move as fast as I thought it would. The next pair of disused lines it checks out just yield sixty years of dirt and more odd graffiti tags.

Bernie suggests we do another quad and then call it a night. "The battery's performance isn't optimal. It should have enough charge for at least the next two quads but it doesn't."

Seb stands up and stretches his back. "One more," he agrees. "This one looks more promising. There are at least five unused bits of track."

"Roger that, I'm switching to quad two."

Ten minutes after the start of our search.

"Did you see that?" Daz's voice startles me. I had zoned out. He hits the pause button and Bernie's voice comes over the coms.

"You found something?"

"Not sure. I thought I saw something flash."

"Stand by. I'm dousing the drone lights and switching to NV mode."

Bernie goes silent. We all look at each other. The minute stretches to two, then three, four. Seb keys the radio.

"Bernie? You read me?"

Silence, then some scratching noises and, "Target acquired!" Bernie's voice rings around the platform. "She's all here. I'm attaching a GPS beacon. Seb, a word, in private."

Seb plugs in the headphones and walks further away from us. We get one end of his conversation with Bernie — all three lines of it.

"How soon can we move it?"

...

"Say again?"

...

"I understand. I'll take it to Pond."

And that's it. Daz and I are summarily dismissed which is an odd feeling for me as I'm normally the one who tells people they can leave.

Daz is happy but frustration is starting to creep in.

"So when do I get my exclusive?" he asks Seb.

"Not yet. There is some work I have to do first."

"What work, man. The train is all there, all there. Just get the railway men to move it back."

Seb scratches the side of his rebuilt (long story, a former colleague used his face as a football) nose. A sign I recognize from when he's trying to decide whether to tell me something.

"Bernie found the train. The missing train had four carriages attached. This one has five."

"An extra carriage. What's the big deal?"

"That carriage has wires, traces of C4 and a human sized hole cut into the floor. Bernie is taking a sample to compare with what was found in Lars Thorsen's room. And I don't care who your father is, if word of this leaks out you'll be spending the useful years of your life in a prison cell."

Daz and I make our way back to the deserted concourse to wait for Bernie and Seb. Daz now complains bitterly. I let him because I'm beginning to think along the lines of the hidden threat under our feet. Since I met Seb, I have become more aware of the constant struggle that goes on in secret. The stuff that makes it into the papers is when things go wrong. When things go right the newspapers never hear a peep. These chaps give a whole new meaning to secret policemen; they keep us safe and we don't even know it. Seb has given me just the tiniest glimpse below the surface of the everyday. Like a parallel world that he and others in the intelligence community inhabit. It only intersects with our world in certain places.

While Daz is whinging about losing his exclusive, which I'm pretty sure he won't, I'm wondering who cut the hole in the floor, and where they were parked, and for how long, and what happened to the explosives. It's a question I'll pose to Seb later.

1 a.m.

I woke up an hour ago, and he was gone, which worries me because he doesn't need to go out in the early hours anymore.

His key rattles in the lock. He comes upstairs and goes straight into the shower. I give him a few minutes. Once the water is running, I get up and pad downstairs to the kitchen to make some coffee. When he reappears I'm sitting in bed cupping a mug, knees drawn up to my chest. He takes the other mug off the tray I've set out for him and loads it with sugar.

The first time I ask, he makes a show of sipping his coffee. The second time he can see I'm not going to stop asking. He's honest with me. He says he 'doesn't know'.

"Why not take just the engine?"

"Pardon?"

"Why take the carriages? What was to be gained from taking all of the carriages?"

"That is what I've been trying to work out. I've jogged around Wandsworth common three times and all I've done is run my mind around in circles. There had to be a reason. I just don't know what it was."

"You want something concrete to give Pond don't you?"

"You can read me like a book sometimes, which is troubling." He puts down his mug.

"Don't tell him you found it yet."

"He'll find out."

"Not unless you tell him." Seb leans back against the headrest, a small shudder goes down his spine as I keep talking. "You know he works on available data. If neither you, nae Bernie, nae I, tell him, he's not going to know. Until you're ready to tell him."

"What would that gain us? Thorsen's obviously planted a bomb. We have no way of knowing exactly where. But the Houses of Parliament seem like a safe bet and we have even less time because this year the 5th falls on a Saturday so our deadline is the 4th."

He's keeping something back, I can feel it.

"My gut instinct tells me that Thorsen wanted us to locate the train."

"I dunno, hen. He'd hidden it pretty well."

"He told Coltrane that the 'heavy mob' would be coming to question him. He knew we'd find the thing eventually. And how much time and resources have we wasted locating what is essentially a dumb witness?"

"The second dumb witness," I agree, "The first being Coltrane for staying put after Thorsen's death. I mean how loyal slash stupid is Coltrane? If a mate of mine had set this bomb plot in motion and popped his clogs, I wouldn't have waited around for the police (sic) to show up on ma doorstep and possibly stick me in jail because they couldn't charge Thorsen. Me? I'd have been on the first plane to a non-extradition country."

"Well we don't know the nature of their relationship," Seb stretches and follows up with long drawn-out yawn. "There may be other accomplices keeping tabs on Coltrane, which is why he didn't run.

"I met with Pond this morning." Seb can't see me frowning in the dark, "I've convinced him that some house to house enquiries could provide more leads, or a suspect. So tomorrow morning a team of police will descend on Plumpton Crescent.

"We'll see who talks, and who doesn't. It's also possible Thorsen and Coltrane were lovers."

"Nah," I say. "Coltrane didn't look like he was grieving for anyone. And if it comes out that he and Thorsen were hot and heavy with each other, I'll donate a thousand quid to the labour party!"

"Hmmm," he says. "Well we've still got a few more rocks to turn over. Bernie has some people he thinks might be able to help. He's going to talk to them."

"What did Bernie do? For you lot, I mean?"

Seb doesn't reply. I look across to see if he's fallen asleep. He hasn't.

"You told me yourself he's not a techie," I'm letting my thoughts spool out. "He's not vitamin D deficient, and he talks and moves like a military man. Also, Pond is mildly perturbed by him and I didn't think he was bothered by anything."

"Bernie has, shall we say, some very unique skills. He didn't run a desk. We used to use him when all our options had pretty much run out."

"Bernie's the oap version of Liam Neeson?" I joke.

Seb lays flat and closes his eyes. I should too, it's after 2 a.m., and if I don't get any sleep I'll be sporting carry-on under ma eyes.

I turn over and start to doze off. Beside me I can feel him tossing and turning. I can understand his dilemma. Pond brought him in to find the missing tube train. On the one hand he has found it, on the other he has evidence of a far greater danger.

Could I sit on something like that if it meant that people could be hurt, even killed, if I didn't say something? Pond is a hard task master. I don't like the wee bastard because I've seen fer myself how he treats his agents; like pawns on a chess board. Sacrificing them for the good of the country doesn't bring him out in a sweat like it would a normal person. If that's the hallmark of a good leader then maybe I'm not. My da idolizes Churchill and I used to think Churchill was a great leader too until I discovered things about him that prove idols always have feet of clay. Some of the things Churchill did were between him and his conscience, and I hope they weighed heavily on him, because some of his decisions got people killed for no good reason.

4 a.m.

Ma eyes start open. I'm still not familiar with the night noises this house makes but there's this one floorboard in the kitchen that I call the 'frogboard' because the blasted thing croaks every time I step on it and it just 'croaked'. I look across to see if Seb heard it too. He's cocooned in the duvet just the top of the pillow sticking out. I put my hand over the covers and they're warm so he's buried in there. Careful not to wake him, I grope around on the floor for my tracksuit, put on the jacket, and after a brief struggle, the bottoms. Then I go onto the landing and look down. There's light spilling out from the kitchen and through the bannisters. I can see that the deadbolt and chains that Bernie secures each night are still in place.

Bernie sits at the kitchen table, a half filled glass in front of him. Next to it another clean empty glass and a bottle of Dewars, Seb's favourite brand before we met. Bernie has a Biro in his hand and a copy of yesterday's Daily Mail; open to the puzzle page.

"You're up early," I say.

"Getting old'll do that for you." Bernie picks up the glass, takes a nip. "I barely sleep at all these days."

"Mind if I join you?"

He nods and I pull out the chair opposite him.

"What's bothering you?" Bernie asks. He points to the glass.

"Nae, thanks. And why would anything be botherin' me. I'm fine."

"M'dear," Bernie fixes his gaze on me, "the last time you and Seb had a 'disagreement' you went banging out of here early morning, and now you 'can't sleep'."

"I heard a noise," I say, way too defensively.

"You could've stayed upstairs, instead you're here. And with respect, I've known the lad much longer than you. What did you 'disagree' on this time?"

"We didn't argue, we talked. But I don't think he was completely honest with me."

"About what?"

"I dunno!" I get up and push the kitchen door to. "If I knew I'd call him on it."

"He's a spy, Mary. We have PhDs in deception and degrees in manipulation. And a small black hole where our conscience used to be. Or that could just be me. Our stock in trade is information, acquiring it, dealing in it, holding it over people to get them to do what we want. From a business standpoint we're the insider traders. Our 'shares' have brief value and we have to know when to unload them."

"Appreciate the analogy, hen. But what would you do in his position?"

Bernie drains his scotch, "I'd trade the location of the train for another favour from Pond." He holds up his hands, "You asked what *I* would do. Seb might've done something else."

The words 'house to house enquiries' leap into my mind. So that's how he convinced Pond to help out.

"Whatever he's done, I think he's made a mistake. Pond isn't on his side."

"Mary, it's his mistake to make, not yours."

Bernie's right, damn him, and in a way I'm glad Seb lied because the truth would've led to a blazing row.

'I'm going back to bed."

Climbing back up the stairs, I weigh my reaction. Aye, I'm angry with Seb but I *care* about him. After only six months, I may even be in love with him.

I think his weak spot is Pond, and mine too.

"Seb?"

No answer. He's still wrapped in the duvet, his back facing me. An experimental tug of the covers causes him to roll into the dip in the mattress. He flounders half-awake then rewraps himself. I curl up on my side, pull the hoodie up over my ears and balance at the edge.

CHAPTER 14

Seb was gone when I woke up this morning. The radio is saying that perhaps the UXBs will be made safe today. Bernie is busy in the kitchen when I come down; rounds of toast dealt around the table. In my downtime yesterday I managed to nip over to the high street and buy a couple of office appropriate shirts and some wide legged trousers that move with a satisfying 'swish'. Those tracksuit bottoms were starting to feel a little too clingy.

"He's gone," I indicate the third plate, "and I'll be off in a mo. It would raise all kinds of office eyebrows if they saw me coming out of next door." I grab my plate and spread some butter on ma toast.

"At least if the two of you have another barney you've got somewhere to sleep," says Bernie.

"I've no even been upstairs. There could be a family of eight living up there for all I know."

Day three at the Wandsworth office starts with a bit of good news; P-Gate has been averted. Harrington-Smythe has agreed to terms. Garrett's phone call is brief and makes it plain that he's taking the credit for all this.

I tell him to call Nico Castro and give him the good news. If he wants the credit he'll have to counter any last minute bargains Nico may come up with. I *don't* tell him that I'd expected him to pull something like this.

The work day started with an impromptu meeting and a small revolt. I thought when I broke the news that we might be heading back to central London sooner than expected it would make the staff happy. It didn't.

A small selection of their gripes:

"I like it here."

I'm with *people* not shut up in a cube office."

It's heaven being able to walk over to a desk, not up three flights of stairs and along multiple corridors. I think we should stay out here."

Philly patiently explains that we can't have two head offices. "Besides," she finishes, "the board would think we were staging a coup."

"My boss took his two weeks vacay," says one.

"So did mine," says another.

"Okay!" I raise my voice to quiet them down. "We don't know when the office will reopen, but when it does I don't want to be shuttling between here and there. So, when HQ reopens we'll be moving back there."

Several groans.

"But let's work on making more co-operative work spaces at HQ. Something midway between open plan and cubicles. We'll need to utilize sound absorbent materials or else we'll descend into a bloody tower of babel. The board can keep their offices. It'll only isolate them further, but of course none of them will see it that way."

My phone plays 'the Ipcress File', Seb's ring tone.

"I have to take this. Meeting over."

Several interested stares follow me back to my desk.

"Hey, I'm at the office."

"One of the delights of open plan, having to encode your every word," says Seb. *One we didn't think of.* "Sorry for nicking the covers."

"Making any headway, hen?"

"Yes, but first I have a confession to make."

"I know what you did."

"You do?"

"Aye, you said I could read you like a book. I can also read between the lines." I'd like to say something a little stronger but in this case the prying ears nearby are a blessing not a curse.

"Remember those house to house enquiries I told you about?"

"Aye."

"They've turned up something interesting. You know I thought Coltrane and Thorsen might be lovers?"

"You said it was possible they were. They're nae!" I say, loud enough to draw a glance from Jo.

"Not them, according to a very helpful postman and several neighbours, Thorsen was *very* friendly with his next door neighbour, one Lavinia Worthington."

"And what does she have to say for herself?"

"She isn't talking, which is suspicious, I sent a constable over to talk to her and she sent him packing. Refused to let him in."

"Is there a Mr. Worthington?"

"She's a widow, and the people in the street thought it was good that she and Thorsen were discreetly getting together."

"Is your merry widow retired?"

I sense a change in his voice, a hint of excitement. "I thought you'd never ask. According to our enquiries no one knows *exactly* what she does but the consensus is she's some kind of civil servant."

"Parliamentary?"

"Hard to say, but she's got that Whitehall mentality off to a tee. I experienced it for myself. I used my MI6 credentials, thinking I could overawe her. It didn't work.

"The old battle axe refused to talk to me, wouldn't let me into her house, claimed she had a dentist's appointment. I can see her walking back from the bus stop now. Look, I need a favour. I'm taking my postie witness in. Can you come over and try to get Worthington to talk? I know it's a lot to ask."

"It *is* a lot to ask, hen. I cannae just drop everything every time you need a favour. That being said, I do need to check on the situation at HQ. I suppose I could take a detour. Where are you?"

"Number 40 Plumpton Crescent, Wimbledon. Thorsen lives, lived at number 42."

I scribble down the addresses.

"I'll make it up to you. Pond's given me a DC from the Met to keep an eye on any comings and goings. I'll tell the chap that you'll be here. When? Soon?"

"Don't push your luck, hen." I ring off and then whilst the information is still fresh in my mind I rewrite it, printing so that I can read my own handwriting.

"Jo, order me a taxi would you?"

I read off the unfamiliar Plumpton Crescent address and she picks up the phone without batting an eyelid.

"Alex, could I have a word?"

I should join cirque de soleil, two balls in the air, no problem——along with one possible hand grenade all set to blow up in my face.

"Walk with me, Alex."

"If I must," he says in that Eton-esque drawl of his. Alex is a sharp dresser. Nothing off the peg for him, Paul Smith shirts and techie ties. This one has a NASA logo on it. He's a lesser freckled ginger with green eyes big enough to give him the look of a character from a manga comic.

"I've been re-reading your file. You made it plain you wanted to work at Loch-Maccallans for the long haul. Garrett made a note to offer you the next seat on the board when it came free. You still interested?"

He nods his reply, then, "Which one of them do I have to kill?"

If only murder were an option.

"There will be a seat coming free, soon."

"This wouldn't have anything to do with Castro would it?"

"I cannae tell you any more than I have. Just know there's no foul play involved. If you are interested, I'm going to use my influence to put you up for it."

"Why?"

"Because I want there to be a company by the time you retire. Garrett brought these guys onto the board when they were young and hungry. Now they're old and crusty and in two to three years' time they will start retiring. If natural causes don't get them first."

"Our lack of direction has been noted."

"I want to get us off the blunt edge onto the one that bleeds. I've been outvoted more times than I even want to think about. Putting you on the board would shake things up. We make a great product, but our marketing is hit and miss. We don't use new technology effectively, and we sure as hell haven't changed our manufacturing processes in a decade."

"You don't have to pitch me that. I know. So, you think I'll be in your pocket if you get me on the board?"

"Nae, Alex. I'd just want you to vote for what's best for the company, not the shareholders. Sometimes that would mean agreeing with me, sometimes not. I was looking through your interviews before, and da made some very detailed comments. Several times he noted your integrity; underlined them even. There are plenty of candidates to fill that board position who could do the job, but da recognized something in you; a quality that *he* had when he joined this company. He sensed you could do the job with integrity."

"I'm interested," Alex drawls. "I seem to remember from the articles that it requires four existing members to sponsor a new board member. You'll be lucky if you can scrape up one."

"I won't be doing the sponsoring, da will. And if we get you in, Alex, make no mistake, you and I will butt heads. I may even waste my vote a few times by voting against you. Being independent of me is a good way to shepherd the others in the right direction."

For a second I think Alex is impressed, then he puts a hand over his mouth to cover a short burp.

"Do I have to throw my name in the hat?"

"You don't have to do *anything* for now. Just be ready, and for god's sake act surprised when they call you in."

"I've got a trip with my girlfriend this weekend. Should I postpone it?"

He's pushing the envelope, asking for specifics.

"The next board meeting is Monday morning, UXB permitting. So no, don't cancel any travel plans."

My taxi pulls up and I leave him on the pavement looking thoughtful.

I give the driver the address and sit back. Now, how to tackle an old battle axe?

It's hard to come up with a workable strategy for dealing with someone you've never met. At parties I tend to be a giant ear on legs, staying away from the loud talkers because as the saying goes *empty vessels make the most noise*. If people ask me what I do, straight from the 'how to meet people at parties handbook', I just say I run a small haggis importers and move on before their eyes begin to glaze over.

The taxi driver is using that strange sixth sense that a few of them have. We are heading towards Wimbledon except he doesn't always follow the signposted route. I make a note of a few clever shortcuts he takes, including one through a Waitrose car park that cuts off a notorious set of traffic lights, notorious to me because I've never sailed through them on green.

I wanted the taxi to drop me at the top of the road. A very dogged learner driver puts paid to that. One brake tap from the taxi and the learner and his instructor will be joining me.

"Look at this muppet!" The taxi driver calls back. "If 'e finks e's doin' a three point turn dahn 'ere, e's a few sandwiches short of a picnic if you arske me."

"Drop me outside number 42," I say, reaching for my wallet. The taxi pulls smoothly off into a double space where a fire hydrant sits flush with the front of the taxi. The learner crawls past.

"All paid for, love," says the driver. "Bird that ordered paid with a company card. You're all set."

Bless Jo. I pass a tip to the driver and slide out. He and the learner keep going, vanishing as they both turn a corner.

Now I have to stop thinking like a CEO and start thinking like Seb. A civilian would just go up to the front door and knock or go straight in. Seb said there was a man keeping an eye on the place so I should check in with him first. There's only one car occupied. I go over and tap on the window. He lowers his red masted scandal sheet. On the seat beside him a giant open thermos and a navy blue police issue pullover.

"Mary Maccallan." I show him my driver's license, feeling faintly ridiculous.

He checks it, looks at me and back at the picture on the license again.

"Your Boss said you were coming. The place is unlocked. Just go in. He said not to touch anything inside."

He said nothing of the sort to me, ya jumped up. Patience Mary, patience.

"Has Worthington come back?"

"Haven't seen her." He goes back to his paper which, unless he cut eyeholes in it, would be impossible to see through.

"Is she at number 40 or 44?"

"40."

Number 42 is empty. It's already starting to feel unlived in. Because DC woodentop told me not to touch anything, I nosey around the downstairs. Expecting to find books on Guy Fawkes, Thorsen's special subject bordering on obsession. Instead I find a typical bachelor pad: big screen TV, games console, games, giant sofa sans cushions, football scarves for Man U and Arsenal, lots of action movies on DVD, a pool table, cases of Heineken, and a crate of wheat beer with an odd name. Not a single book, not even magazines. One or the other, maybe both, are pathologically tidy. The kitchen is showroom ready. Upstairs the tidiness continues; Thorsen's room: curtains drawn, books, maps, a fiercer tidiness. Calendar on the wall has a familiar date circled. Seb's people have been in and removed the explosives, leaving a single brown paper wrapper behind with the words: Block, demolition, M4 (Composition C4).

Stenciled underneath, a lot number, and date and year of manufacture, 1999.

The paper smells faintly of something resembling engine oil. I'm careful not to touch it, and move on to Coltrane's room. His curtains are pulled open. The room has a base note of old spice and stilton socks. The view down into their back garden shows more concrete than grass. Butted up against the fence, on Mrs. Worthington's side, someone has placed an incinerator. Something protrudes from the top.

In Mrs. Worthington's garden is a forest of snow white sheets hung out to dry. If she comes out to check on them I might be able to have a chat with her.

The back door is locked. Conveniently, a key dangles from a hook. Up against the outside kitchen wall stands a battered BBQ and a pair of not much better condition patio chairs. The wind picks up, sending the galleon of sheets next door into full sail. No sign of Worthington. The incinerator has a white plastic bowl on top of it. This is what caught my attention from the window. WORTHINGTON is scrawled across the bottom.

"Haven't seen you around here before." I can hear her but not see her. Lavinia Worthington, masked by the sheets, makes her way through them and over to the fence. She has a 'determined posh' look about her. Sleeps in curlers most likely to get that lacquered helmet look, and her voice is probably more brassy when not speaking to strangers like me. I've seen her type before. The 'ministry wives' is what my godfather Charlie calls them; a team of capable, hard-nosed and utterly unswervable females who keep the older ministers in check. Governments come and go but ministry wives and the mandarins of Whitehall keep the country ticking over.

"No," I say, putting out a hand, not sure if she'll take it. "I'm Mary."

"Lavinia, or as your boss calls me, the old battle axe next door."

I can't help a quick smile at that. Seb needs to be more careful. "He's not my boss."

"Oh, you're one of them independent women I keep hearing about. You lot still burning your bras?"

I shake my head. "I burned my bra," says Worthington, "and I marched. Know what I got? Droopy boobs."

"Your neighbours say you're some kind of civil servant. Trying to work on the system from the inside these days?"

Her turn to smile, but she doesn't answer my question. Instead she asks, "So what's happened to that lovely Mr. Thorsen? I saw the rat he shares with being taken away yesterday."

"Mr. Thorsen had an accident, fatal I'm afraid."

Worthington gives a tiny squeak, like she stood on a hamster.

I keep talking while she dabs at her eyes with a paper hankie.

"We've been interviewing all of Mr. Thorsen's neighbours. My colleague tried to tell you what was going on. We've managed to keep the press away from the story but these things have a habit of getting out in unexpected ways."

"Quite. Um... I'm feeling a little odd. I'll go and have a sit down and some tea."

"Do you want me to come over?"

"I'm not an invalid," Worthington growls. "Wait there where I can keep an eye on you."

CHAPTER 15

I look at the incinerator, speculating that if it was alight the wind would have blown sooty smoke all over Lavinia Worthington's pegged out laundry. An idea starts to form. I go back towards the kitchen and take the rusted BBQ tongs from the lid of the grill. The serrated edges allow me to pry up the plastic bowl to get a look inside the incinerator. Worthington would've seen Coltrane, 'the rat', from her kitchen window. She acted quickly, I'll give her that. Some of the papers he was burning have barely caught although the ink has run on the top set. I ease the lid back down, well aware that me poking around in there could do more harm than good. I might destroy something important.

Seb answers on the second ring. "Hang on." He covers the receiver so I get a muffled, "Keep going, I'll be back in a moment."

"Hello, you," he says. He's not in a private area, there are muffled voices and sounds of running feet. "I'm at Paddington Green again, with the helpful postie."

"I've spoken to Mrs. Worthington." I quickly outline what was said and then ask, "The day you scooped up Coltrane did you see anything burning in the back garden?"

"No," Seb pauses. "I surprised him when he came in the back door."

"You should be nicer to Mrs. Worthington, hen," I say. "She doused whatever Coltrane was burning with her washing up water. She wasn't doing it to help you, but to save her wash. Anyway, a lot of what he was trying to torch didn't get burnt."

"I'll send our nerd squad over." Seb says, excitement sparking in his voice. "This could be the break we've been looking for. Listen, I have to get back. We'll celebrate tonight." He blows a kiss down the phone. 'I'll be sure to let Pond know you found a good lead, it'll annoy him no end."

As I hang up Lavinia approaches, her cheeks freshly powdered, eyes still a little damp, a little steadier on her feet than when she left.

"Still here then."

I nod, refusing to take any offense at her rudeness. "I have a couple of questions."

"And it'll be only couple of questions. My bus will be here shortly, so get on with it."

"How well did you know Lars Thorsen?"

"We were friends. He and I have become quite close since my Bert died."

"Were you lovers?"

"That's none of your beeswax. Are you sure it was an accident?" she asks, "I wouldn't put anything past Coltrane."

"I'm told Thorsen slipped and fell prey to the third rail."

"I can't help wishing it had been Coltrane. He's lazy. He works nights I know, they both do, did, do, but Lars didn't need to take a lodger, he was already working two jobs."

"Two jobs?" I say, noting the sigh as she says Thorsen's first name. I wonder wryly what the merry widow had in mind.

"Where do you work, Lavinia?"

"Goodness," Worthington is looking at her watch. "My bus'll be along any moment." She bustles away still talking. "I hate being late."

And with that she's gone. Moments later I hear her front door slam and the grinding arrival of a bus.

I want to go after her, but I wait until the so called nerd squad arrives and seals the incinerator inside a massive blue plastic container. When they've gone, I fish out my Oyster card and go to the bus stop. The 57 trundles up. I tap on, then get off at Raynes Park and take the train to Vauxhall. I'm turned back at the bridge, so that answers that question.

I take the tube back to Wandsworth and the train overground to Wandsworth Common. Making a quick stop at Café Nervosa, I eat my lunch on the bench next to the duck pond. The phone rings in my pocket. "Hello?"

"Hi." The voice on the other end is new to me. "Mizzz Maccallan?"

"Aye?"

"This is Mandy with show bookings dot uk. You signed up to attend the Stupendioso Magic Show tonight?"

"I did." Weeks ago and the tickets are pinned to the cork board in my flat. "I don't have the tickets though, they're stuck in the blast zone."

"We've had to move the venue, so that won't be a problem." She reels off a code. "This replaces your pair of tickets."

"I don't have a pen. Can you text that to me?"

She reads me my phone number and then the details of the revised venue. Moments later my phone buzzes as the text arrives.

"The show will start at 7 p.m. sharp. We're waiving the evening dress requirement."

"Thanks."

6:30:

I'm in a cab on my way to the 'Festival Rooms' out Teddington way. I was wondering why the cabbie smirked when I gave him the address; now, pulling up outside the venue I can see why. The name is a bit posh for what is essentially a village hall.

Daz is my companion for the evening. Seb and Bernie are busy following Thorsen's trail. Bernie has

come up with a nickname for him, 'the Norse nut-
ter', or 'NN' within earshot of civilians or Seb's
former colleagues.

I pay the driver and find Daz leaning against his
bike. "I looked this guy up on Time Out's website
and he got great reviews," he says, "but if you don't
want to get up on stage, stay out of the front four
rows."

"I feel like living dangerously," I say, crossing the
road and tacking onto the back of the line going into
the 'festival rooms'. The men and women on the
door simply ask for the code Mandy from Show
Bookings texted me. They feed it into a little
handheld device and it beeps; the white light at the
front turning green.

Daz and I take the fourth row on the end. Late-
comers are the ones who end up having to take the
seats ahead of us. Exactly on time, the lights dim.
The stage, that is more used to having local theatre
companies and tea dances, has been spiffed up; as
soon as the curtains open the unmistakable waft of
fresh paint drifts into the audience.

"Welcome!" a voice booms over the PA system.
"Ladies and gentlemen, boys and girls, may we present to you, Stupendioso!" And out he walks in his

underpants. The audience falls about laughing as his assistant bounds out of the wings with a massive black velvety cloak over one arm. She swathes her magician in it and causes a further riot when he turns away from us, showing the words, MAN AT VOLDERMORT, on the back in at least 250 point font. His first trick is getting dressed. Somehow he managed to put clothes on while coaxing an audience member onto the stage.

"I am Stupendioso. My friends call me Stupes, and this is why." He hands the volunteer a megaphone. "On the count of three, I want you to yell STUPES DOWN! Can you do that for me, my love?

"Shortening my name has saved me in many an altercation. Allow us to demonstrate. Ready, my love?"

The volunteer nods and on three she bawls into the megaphone. Stupes would've been deaf in one ear had he still been next to her, but he's gone! I saw him throw the sleeves of his cloak into the air, hands slipping through, and his head dropping through the neck of the cloak. The garment seems to stand on its own for a fraction of a second before collapsing empty to the ground. The volunteer can't help herself; she pokes the cloak with her shoe. The lights dip causing a gasp from the audience. On our row a latecomer is pushing his way along the line, whispering 'scuse me, pardon me, scuse me'. A single spotlight shines down illuminating our late arrival as Stupes. Another gasp and plenty of applause.

Back on stage, he continues.

"Righto. I'm going to make a bet with you lovely people. I'll be showing you how this trick is done but you'll all have to concentrate very hard to catch me in the act. Now to show there's no jiggery-pokery, I will select a volunteer. You sir," he says pointing at Daz, who points at himself. "Yes." Stupes laughs. "The splendid Indian gent with his finger in his chest." More laughter. "Come on up."

Daz clambers up the makeshift stairs onto the stage. Soon he is sitting on a stool with a box of Man sized Kleenex on his lap. Stupes, standing behind Daz, places a finger on his lips.

"Right. What's your name, sir?"

"Daz."

"Well, Daz, keep your eyes on me." Stupes stands beside Daz, points to his chest, where his hands currently are. "Eyes on me, keep watching my hands, remember son you're keeping me honest."

Daz keeps his gaze on the magician's hands. Stupes pulls a tissue out and balls it up. "Eyes on me, Daz. One, two, (the ball flies over Daz's head) three! Which hand is it in?"

There are titters from the audience. Stupes again puts a finger to his lips. He continues to make bigger and bigger balls of wadded up tissues vanish by throwing them over Daz's head. Each time he tells Daz to 'never take your eyes off my hands', while he keeps pointing to the area in front of his chest, ensuring that Daz keeps his gaze fixed there. The assistant comes out with a broom and sweeps all the tissues to the side. We're all in on the trick. The magician has included us, and no one feels the need to yell out to Daz that the tissues are behind him. For his piece de resistance, Stupes takes the tissue box crumples it into a ball, and as he tosses it aloft, the assistant catches it and takes herself and the broom off stage. As Daz is taking his bows, Stupes stuffs a few tissues into his jacket pockets for him to find later.

CHAPTER 16

November 2nd:
The WWII bombs have gone. They were airlifted out last night. The whole thing managed to stay hush, hush. They didn't want to scare the bejesus out of Londoners by saying bombs might be exploding around them while they slept. This time when I get to Vauxhall I can walk over to our offices. There's a bit of a carnival atmosphere, shops and restaurants are advertising 'We're UXB FREE! specials'. None of the Wandsworth branch came with me, not even Jo. Once inside the Loch-Maccallan building, I run a quick inventory of the equipment and the offices. Everything seems to be in order. I quickly retrieve the fax sent by Harrington-Smythe, which for some reason only it knows, didn't come through to the Wandsworth branch. I

had a chat with Alex this morning and he's ready for operation 'hoodwink the board'. Literally no one else is here. The office cleaners will be in tonight. They have been calling us every day that they couldn't get in. Sitting in my office feels odd.

Lunchtime I have to lock up the whole building because it's still just me. I join the throng of people who are walking towards the Thames, and before I know it the towers of the Palace of Westminster are looming over me. There are police *everywhere*. From the air they must look like luminous, swarming, yellow ants.

In order to avoid the tourists, I cross to the other side of Parliament Street, passing the dove grey, imposing buildings that line the route to the Cenotaph (which I mispronounced as 'Cem-o-taff' before moving here). Now I'm in Whitehall and still find nothing food related. I was just thinking that there must be massive canteens behind these stone walls when I see Lavinia Worthington coming out of The Clarence bar. She's surrounded by a small pack of sloanes, all twentysomethings with the graceful builds of thoroughbreds and the sleek blonde manes to match. Another girl, closer to my age but with Lavinia's fashion sense, brings up the rear. Lavinia

and her companion shepherd the girls past the statue of the Duke of Cambridge on horseback, and
further down, also mounted, Earl Haigh. I lose sight
of them after the WWII women's memorial, which
doesn't feel like any women were involved in its design; one of the hats and coats in the right light
looks like a cross between a spaceman and Top
Gear's Stig. There are people and tour busses all up
and down the road.

I didn't see which building Lavinia and her
troupe of performing sloanes ended up going into so
that's that. I did what Seb asked me to do. Went
above and beyond, actually.

"Hey hen, it's me, can you talk?"

"I'm between meetings, or sit down panic ses-
sions, to give them a better description."

"I don't know if it has any bearing but I ran across
Worthington again today. You were right. She does
work in Whitehall."

"Where in Whitehall?" The strain he's under
shows in the clip in his voice. "Parliament?"

"No, further down. I didn't see which building
she went into but she came out of the Clarence with

a bunch of other 'gels'. Did you have any joy with Coltrane's failed self-destruct?"

"The nerd squad are reconstructing that stuff from the incinerator. Worthington's water did a great job of killing the fire, but it ruined most of Thorsen's hand-written notes. We did find the remnants of an ID badge and an emergency procedures sign. And a rather soggy clipboard. They were soaked in meths to make sure they got torched first."

"Damn."

"Worthington bothers me. She and Thorsen wouldn't exactly move in the same circles. He only had two memberships, the railway workers union, and a bowling team. Lavinia Worthington doesn't crop up in his background anywhere."

"Maybe they met at work?"

"I doubt that. Thorsen's hardly the civil servant type. Plus, he was born in Norway. He'd have to go through a ton of background checks in order to work anywhere sensitive, especially in Whitehall. Meaning I'd be able to pull his security clearance and we'd have a file on him."

"Hmmmnn."

"What? You have an idea?"

"Oh, nae, hen, just thinking out loud."

"Mary, I have to go. I'll see if I can send someone over to the Clarence to interview the bar staff and show them a picture of Thorsen. They hear stuff sometimes. I mean he may have hung around in the Clarence."

"What, like a fox waiting for a plump and juicy civil servant to come to him? If he walked up to her in a place like that where she's in her element, and at her most intimidating, she'd treat him like chewing gum stuck on the sole of her shoe."

"Right now I'm willing to explore every avenue."

"Kay, hen. I'm going to stay in the flat tonight. The office will open up again tomorrow. The Wandsworth branch was useful while it lasted."

"I might come by later. Depends on how things are going here."

Later:

The flat was big and empty. And I admit it, the puzzle of how Worthington and Thorsen crossed paths has been bugging the hell out of me.

I retrace my steps from earlier, still keeping the suit on, and push through the door of the Clarence. A wave of noise washes over me. A glut of different conversations all going at once. In order to talk to one another, customers have to have their faces pretty close. The steel and glass construction of the place bounces the sound around, magnifying it. The place is crammed. Most of those standing up are trying to get drinks. I get a peek at the bar and see all the seats are taken. This was a bad idea. As I turn to leave, I bump straight into the girl that was with Worthington at lunchtime. She's clutching something in her hand, and it falls to the ground in a rainbow of colours.

She gives a small bleat of distress and we both scrabble on the ground for it. I get there first. It's a government ID with all the holograms, similar to the one Seb used to carry.

"Here," I hand it back to her. "You don't want to lose that."

"No, I do not."

"Good luck in there," I say. "It's the world's worst game of sardines."

She looks past me and shudders. "Crap-on-a-shitsicle." Only the English can curse in those plummy vowels and get away with it.

"Didn't I see you with Lavinia earlier?" It's a gamble, I know, and it may backfire, but I'll never know if I don't try.

"Yes, I'm her deputy, Poppy."

"Well, it was nice to meet you, Poppy. I'm Mary, Mary Snow. I couldn't get a drink so I guess I'll go and find a karaoke bar."

"There are karaoke bars around here?" She hiccups the 'gosh'.

"Not around here. It would be entertaining catching a cabinet minister or a faceless civil servant belting out Tina Turner ballads, but, no. The bar I have in mind is over towards Shaftesbury Avenue. They are less inhibited over there, and with the day I've had..."

"I've never done karaoke before. Is it hard?"

"Not after a few drinks. It's the best stress reliever."

A flicker of suspicion crosses Poppy's face. "You work in Whitehall?"

"Nae, hen, I work in Victoria. I live out Wimbledon way. Just burning off some steam before I get the tube home."

"I'd love to try karaoke," Poppy says, a longing in her voice.

I'm sure in the spy infiltration handbook under 'get to know your target' it says something along the lines of *you should ask them to come with you,* but something stops me. I know now which building Worthington works in, and Poppy's not as adorably clueless as she seems at first glance.

"Grab a gang of friends and head over there. It's called Kashu, just off Romilly street. It was nice to meet you, Poppy."

"You too, Mary."

I walk back up Whitehall, retracing my steps, past Parliament, skirting the large contingent of police,

"Excuse me, Miss." A large yellow roadblock stands in front of me. I nearly cannon into him because I want to get back to the flat and call Seb. "Come with me please. Someone would like a word." He raises the yellow tape and I feel a hand on my back pushing me through. I'm swamped——the meat in a Met sandwich. I know how the card feels in a game of 'find the lady'.

"I'm surprised at you, Maccallan." Pond, of course it's bloody Pond. For someone I can't stand he's been cropping up far too much. "Miller sent you snooping and thought I wouldn't notice."

"Snooping?" I go the full Scottish, "Snooooooo-pin'. I was walkin' back to ma flat, you wazzoch!"

"You've no business being in this area."

"I wis meetin' a friend for a drink in the Clarence."

"Name?"

"Vinnie Worthington."

"Of the Wimbledon Worthington's?" Pond raises a hairy eyebrow. I double speak like this with Seb all the time when we're out in public. Having the head of MI6 do it makes me slightly nauseous. I assumed, wrongly, that Seb would keep his newest discoveries away from Pond for now, but the man cannae resist sharing.

"Aye, she wasn't there. The place was stuffed. I was going home and then you had me reeled in from across the road. I did nae ask to be marinated in testosterone. Can I go now?"

"You're hiding something. I can smell it."

"Nae Pond, that's just your aftershave."

"Officers," he summons the met sandwich who have been standing a feet few away. "Escort this woman off the premises, and if you see her in this area again during the duration of this operation, arrest her."

"Pond, never a pleasure." To the officers, "I'll take my police escort now." I follow the two bemused officers back to the yellow tape. They raise it. "Thanks, hens." I duck under. The tape swishes down my back as it falls. There's an ITV reporter doing a piece to camera directly in my path. He muffs his lines and goes for another take, giving me the opportunity to nip behind him and continue back towards the flat.

The street lamps are on along the Thames. There's an odd calm settled over the city. My phone Ipcresses, and that's no a word you'll find in the English dictionary.

"Hen?"

"What did you do, Mary? I just had Pond on the phone threatening to stick you behind bars."

"Ooch, he's just being a dickheid. He's got it into his noggin that I'm spying on him for you."

"That's ridiculous!"

"That's what I told him."

"What *were* you doing down there?"

I check behind me. *Since when did I get so paranoid?* People are walking but no one close to me. I shield the mic with my hand and tell him the truth.

"You think Worthington's an accessory?"

"Nae. Well I don't think so. Why would she risk a life-long civil service career and pension for Thorsen?"

"Beats me but you've given me an idea. Everyone associated with Thorsen is in watertight compartments of his making. I wonder how they feel about each other?"

It's a rhetorical question. Seb sometimes wanders around the flat muttering to himself. It's a good job Pond hasn't thought to try and bug the place. He'd think Seb was losing his marbles.

"I might be able to use one to crack the other."

"And there I think I can help." Again I casually scan the immediate area. "I know what Worthington's job title is and more importantly which building she works in."

"I'm listening."

"I ran into Poppy Cho-mond-ley," I spell it.

"It's pronounced Chum-leigh," Seb corrects.

"Why can't you sassenachs spell things correctly?" I grouse. "You're all full of bloody Sin Jins and Towcesters. Say St John and Toaster and I'd be fine, and it's Mary Magdalen not Maudlin."

"Poppy Chumleigh?"

I tell him about the dropped holographic ID.

"Poppy is Worthington's deputy. Worthington is head of the archivist division at the Inland Revenue building on Whitehall."

"Now *that* I can work with. Do you know how many Worthington's work for HMG? It's a lot. They wouldn't let me run a search of the entire civil service employee records but you just narrowed it down, and I should've realized that she'd be an EO."

"EO?"

"Executive Officer. Chumleigh's probably an admin officer."

"You're speaking Greek, hen."

His phone double beeps.

"Hang on, I'm getting another call. I'll call you back."

He hasn't called by the time I get back to the flat. It's only when I'm in my pj's drifting off snug in my own bed that I realize that.

Nov 3rd:

The Wandsworth Branch remains open. Luckily no one else has noticed. There's enough of a spread of people who took advantage of the UXBs to go off on last minute vacations. Jo is back at her desk. I called Alex and told him that they can stay there until Friday because we only have the lease until then; a little white lie but a seemingly effective one. Not a word from Seb since last night.

I've just come off a conference call with da and am on my way to retrieve the company paperwork I stashed in the Mailboxes Are Us. Without even thinking about it I cut through Whitehall. It was only when I saw the Spire of the Palace of Westminster that I realized my mistake. Pond may have been bluffing about having me put on ice, but I'm not taking that chance. There's a bus stop on the other side of the road in front of the Customs and Excise Building, which I now know to also house the Inland Revenue. I can take the next bus a few stops and avoid having to backtrack. The traffic is stationary, mostly tourist buses with a smattering of cars and a couple of vans. When I get off, I check to make sure the driver of the van closest to the kerb has seen me, and my mouth drops open. Sitting beside the driver is Bernie, unmistakable in one of his trademark Hawaiians. The side door slides open and Seb gets out, his back to me. He fiddles with his ear, tapping it twice, then crosses to the entrance of the Revenue building and flashes his ID at the policeman in yellow flouro guarding the door. I can't follow him. The van pulls away, Bernie watching from the side mirror. The van takes a left vanishing in the direction of the riverfront and the Eye. I wonder what, if anything, Coltrane gave Seb on Worthington. Or is he questioning Worthington to get something to break Coltrane? We're only one day away from Seb's career collapsing like a house of cards.

CHAPTER 17

The van reappears, cruising into the bus lane and pulling to a stop alongside me. "Want a lift, Mary?" Bernie asks, getting out of the passenger side and sliding the rear door open far enough for us both to get in. He slides it shut and off we go. The van parks a few moments later but by then I've been sucked in by what's on the TV in here.

"I called in a couple of favours. Always good to have Pond concerned about keeping in my good books." Bernie chats away about the 'professional courtesy' shown by the security 'bods,' his word not mine, whilst we watch the view from the tiny camera mounted in a button on Seb's lapel.

"We were banking on the equipment not going through their scanners, and like good little bods they fast-tracked him."

Bernie keeps going. I half listen. Some words like 'wi-fi', 'bandwidth', 'tame nerd', and 'boosted signal' land on the shores of my conscious mind. Others just go in one ear and out the other. Like watching the drone's footage a couple of nights ago, it is easy to zone out. Seb is in his element, making small talk with his security escort.

Lift doors swish open revealing more walls, painted in baby poo green.

"Do you know Lars Thorsen?" Seb asks.

Now *that* got my attention.

"Not very well. He worked down in 'the tombs', archive security," the man explains. "Everything is digitized these days, but you know HMG, everything in triplicate. They keep paper copies of the old files in case the computers go down. How do you know him?"

"When he left here he got a job driving tube trains for TFL. He helped me find a missing train recently."

Not exactly a lie.

"He didn't really leave here. He still subs for us. But Mrs. Worthington will be able to tell you more."

Seb knocks and enters. Poppy looks up from her desk and breaks into a smile.

"Gosh," she says, "You must be the man from 'the sandcastle.'"

"Sorry?"

"The MI6 building. We call it the sandcastle. How do you do. I'm Poppy by the way."

"Poppy, I'm Sebastian. Your boss is expecting me."

"Be careful in there," Poppy warns. "She's in a foul mood, I've had my head bitten clean off my shoulders twice already today."

"Does she breathe fire?"

Poppy chortles. Seb has her in the palm of his hand.

"Oh gawd. Do they teach effortless flirting at spy school?"

"He can hear you," Bernie whispers. "It's a two-way earpiece."

Shite.

"Don't look so worried," Poppy says. "Her bark is far worse than her bite."

Seb opens the door and goes in. Worthington is writing something, her head bent towards the desk. He looks around while she keeps him waiting. Filing cabinets stand on either side of her desk. Behind is a wall of certificates, a photo on the desk facing her. Seb dwells for a while on the keypad next to a heavily reinforced door that might break your ankle if you tried kicking it down.

Having established her importance Worthington looks up.

"You!" She doesn't look happy to see him. "I talked to your girl friday. Surely you don't need to keep hounding me. I told her what I know."

"Mrs. Worthington, I came to thank you. Your swift actions preserved some vital evidence that Coltrane was trying to burn. As a result Lars Thorsen is now the focus of our investigation."

"The poor man's dead!"

"The poor man, as you call him, was hoarding bricks of C4. I think he was building a bomb and I think he was using you to keep it hidden."

"Lars Thorsen wasn't capable of building a bomb."

"I have a witness that says different, and that bomb is somewhere in the city right now. It could even be in the archives." Lavinia's eye shows a hint of a tear.

"He wouldn't. He wouldn't hurt us, hurt me. We're his friends."

"We're questioning several people in connection with Thorsen's plans. One of them was asked about your relationship with Thorsen." Seb takes out a small device and pushes the play button.

Coltrane's smug voice echoes around the room. "Oh he cultivated the old bag. He'd go round there and listen to her drivel and eat her food. He hated doing it but he needed her. He even snogged her, said it was like French kissing a corpse, a lavender scented corpse." Seb turns the recorder off. Worthington bows her head and the silence almost seems like a shout. It's very uncomfortable to watch. Then Lavinia raises her gaze to lock with Seb's.

"Coltrane is a liar, a nasty little liar. He's making it all up."

Seb, sounding a little rattled tries another tack. "Then you won't mind showing me 'the tombs'."

"If it'll help to get shot of you," she sighs. "Come with me."

From her desk drawer she extracts a key, jams it into the lock, and with lightening quick fingers keys in a complicated sequence of numbers that not even the camera can follow.

She flips a switch and a warm dim light comes from the desk lamp on the table beside the door. "The tombs."

Our view and Seb's is a single mass divided by the large metal wheels that wouldn't look out of place on a submarine airlock in a disaster movie.

At each end there is a corridor to the wall the same width as the shelving units. The room is massive. Seb takes out a torch and explores the passageways. He even slides around the back where there's a smooth unbroken wall. The only adornment is an emergency sign warning that personnel shouldn't attempt to operate in the tombs alone.

"There's nothing there," I say, forgetting that Seb can hear me.

"Open them," he orders.

Lavinia spins the first wheel and the shelves expand to fill the gap at the side. Seb walks up and down the row examining the cubby holes full of files, steps back out, and repeats the procedure with all twenty four rows. He pulls a few files at random, puts them back.

"Satisfied?" Lavinia asks.

Back in the van I get up to go.

"Tell him to call me, hen. I think he's best left alone for now. He'll be in a foul mood for a bit."

"That he will," Bernie agrees, sliding open the van door to reveal the pedestrian plaza teeming with tourists headed for the London Eye. "The lad doesn't like setbacks, especially when they're witnessed by his peers or loved ones."

I wait until the van is out of sight, then swim upstream, cutting across the back of county hall with the vague idea of sitting in Jubilee Gardens.

Jo calls.

"I've had half a dozen calls from Garrett. He's been trying your phone for the last hour. Did you turn it off?"

"Aye." I turned if off as soon as I got into the van. Bernie insisted.

"Well call him. He...he doesn't sound like himself."

"I'll call him now."

Jo, like the best assistants, can corral me when she needs to. In a way she's the closest thing I have to a ma; not that I'd ever tell her that.

"Da?"

"Is this Miss Maccallan?"

"Aye, and this is my da's phone so where is he?" I demand.

The clinic allows their patients to have unlimited social contact with friends and family. And I've visited a couple of times so that I could check out the level of nursing care and the staff. They are all top notch and I've helped his nurses with subtle suggestions if they thought it would help. But now I'm starting to get a little concerned.

"I'll get him for you." I process the voice. It isn't one I've heard before.

"Mary?"

"Aye, da, sorry you couldn't get hold of me. I was in a meeting, out of the office, way out in the countryside, no phone signals until I hit the M25." I learned a long time ago that when da gets riled by mine or the late Fergus' antics, he vents his spleen over the course of the conversation. To get him a bit more pliable and calmer I always serve my apology straight up with plenty of information and a few lies to boot which usually mollifies the old scroat. If they ever devise a way to track mobile phones I'm in big trouble.

"What is going on, da?"

"Could you leave us, please. I want to talk to my daughter."

I can feel my jaw drop. He *never* calls me his daughter. It's always 'Mary' or 'Lassie'. The only time in living memory that he has called me his daughter was in front of her Majesty at a garden party. I was ten and crammed into a frilly blouse and tartan skirt, da's idea of party attire. I get my fashion nouse from my ma's DNA not his.

"Da, what's wrong?"

"I," his voice goes up a gear, "get out woman. I can see you hovering at the door. Shut it behind ye!"

I hear a muffled 'thump' as the door shuts. The energy leaves his voice.

"Mary, I got the results of my scans this afternoon. It's not good news, lass. The lab grown neurons have been replicating, yet despite how I feel, the scans show that they are shrinking in size and not processing signals to my brain. And worse, they can't stop them replicating. They are overwhelming the healthy cells. I'm being re-written, lass."

"Nooooooo, da. C'mon man that's bollocks. I've seen you on Skype and y'look ten years younger."

"There's no lie lassie.

"I've been over my options with the new specialist and he thinks that there are steps we can take. They're going to stop the stem cell infusions as of tonight. That should slow down the replication process."

"But you'll be back to square one!" I protest, feeling tears spring to ma eyes.

"I will, but I'll still be me. And lassie, I've still got you. You can keep the company moving forward, and I can retire to the Tay wit ma fishing rod."

"Nae, nae, da, aahm no having that. You cannae stop. When I flew out there three months back Dr. Weiss told me he thought you'd be home by Christmas. Get them to retest you."

"He said you'd react like this."

"Doctor Weiss?"

"No, Doctor Orlov."

"Who the fuck is Doctor Orlov?" In the park a passing mother shoots me a sour look for swearing in front of her child.

"My new specialist. Doctor Weiss recommended him. He told me you've met him."

"I most certainly have not!"

"Lass, you have. The last time you visited you had a long meeting with Doctor Orlov. He told me you walked him halfway up the side of a mountain."

"I did'nae!"

Da's voice is now confused, upset, old.

"Ye have!"

"I don't give a flying frog what Doctor Orlov says." Yes, I said 'frog'; the woman is still in earshot. "You tell him I want to talk to him. He's to call me in the next half an hour or I'm on a plane out there. To-night!"

"He's a busy man, lass."

"Da, remember that piece of paper Charlie had you sign. I've got power of attorney over you. If Or-lov doesn't call me, I'm pulling you out of there and I will personally sue his neurological arse back behind the froggin' iron curtain or where ever he comes from. Tell him! Or my next call is to Charlie in Hong Kong. He'll appreciate being woken up at O dark shitty."

"You're over-reactin'."

"Too blood, blasted right I'm over-reacting, and you ain't seen nothing yet, da. This reaction here, this is a squib. If you want the full UXB, hang up on me and see what happens."

"There's no need to shout lass," the tearful tone of voice wenches my heart. I feel like a heel for yelling at him. "I'll have him call you."

"And da, I want to 'see' you next time we talk. Skype me."

I call Seb, not sure if he'll pick up.

"Mary. I was going to call you. Bernie and I just got back to the flat and found it empty."

"I'm on ma way back. I just had some family stuff to deal with."

"Your father?"

"It's no important," I stop myself. I'm doing exactly what got me so angry with him a few days ago. "Actually it is pretty important. My da's had a setback. The scans came back with some pretty strange results," I summarize. "And his new specialist is going to call me back in about fifteen minutes because if he doesn't, Hurricane Mary is going to decimate a Swiss clinic."

"Hurricane Mary. Well, amazing force of nature that you are, Bernie and I are going to make use of your roof garden." In the background I can hear Bernie asking where the good stuff is. "We're going

to try and work out how to stop the late Lars Thorsen from blowing up parliament tomorrow, and
killing my career. If you'd like to join us, I'm sure
you can bring a few valuable insights."

"Pour me a drink. I'm going to walk back. Hopefully I'll have heard from Orlov by then."

My threat worked. Twenty five minutes later on
my way up the stairs to my flat the phone trills in my
pocket, just the standard ring tone.

"Hello?"

"Mary? Doctor Karl Orlov. How pleasant to hear
your voice."

"You've never heard my voice Doctor, and I want
to know what the hell is going on with my da!" Glad I
checked no one was lurking in the stairwell; they
probably heard that in Scotland.

Orlov has the kind of voice that fills the speaker,
inflating like marshmallows in my ears. I can feel a
wave of calm trying to break over me.

"Your father is in rude health. His labs all came
back nominal. His BMP and BP are within toleranc-
es. Our CC is that the neural replication process will
not proceed without external stimuli."

No wonder my da sounded confused!

"So when he said you were stopping the stem cell infusions, he meant they'd already stopped?" I key open the door. A glass of amber scotch on the rocks sits on the coffee table, a note attached.

WE'VE GONE UP TO THE ROOF GARDEN S

Picking up the glass, the rocks clink against each other.

"Correct." Orlov sounds a little miffed and I mentally hi five myself for unravelling part of his jargon laden spiel. All those teenage E.R. marathons finally paid off! "Are you drinking?"

Ignoring his question, I put out one of my own.

"Da told me his brain cells are shrinking, not growing, and he sounded more upset than I've ever heard him." I let the scotch smoulder on the tip of my tongue.

"He is under the impression you are flying out to see him. I wouldn't recommend that course of action."

"Ooch, why not Doc-tor?"

"In my experience, relatives tend to come sallying in armed with advice on how I should treat my patient. They've read of the studies in the Scientific American, the BMJ, or the New England Journal of Medicine, and suddenly they are experts. My twenty years of training, my doctorate, my PhD in neurology, all count for nought."

"Ouch!" I say. Okay, I have read up on the condition my father has, which isn't that well documented. The stem cell information is much more prevalent, and I subscribe to BMJ and NEJ as well as several other online journals. Jingling the ice cubes and taking another nip at the scotch elicits a harrumph of disapproval.

"There is another reason I halted the cell infusions. I've been getting reports from the nurses that interact with Herr Maccallan on a regular basis, and it seems your father has developed some 'traits' which he didn't have when he arrived here."

"Such as?" I take another loud sip and again with the harrumph. Something about me having a drink is getting under his skin. If I can throw him off balance, he might let something slip. "And skip the doc speak or I will be flying out there and I'll be bringing the neurologist da first consulted with as my translator."

"Well, his shellfish allergy has cleared up and he seems to crave human contact; doesn't like being left by himself. Also he hates being in the dark; demands that the lights stay on in his room, resulting in him getting very little sleep."

I find myself nodding. I've seen firsthand what can happen when my da is sleep deprived.

"I Skyped with da last week and he didn't look the least bit sleep deprived."

"It's amazing what caffeine and Visine can do." Orlov injects the tiniest sneer into his voice. Medical professional or not, his arrogant stance is rubbing me up the wrong way.

"Doctor," I cut across him, "please run those tests again. And tell my da the results without the mumbo jumbo."

"Are you telling me how to treat my patient?"

"Nae, Doc, I'm asking you to reassure a frightened old man."

I hang up before he can respond. Not sure what I achieved.

CHAPTER 18

"We're running out of time!" Seb kicks the corner of the patio table. It's not long past seven o'clock. He, Bernie and I are on the roof of the Maccallan's building. Da's veggie patch is a mass of weeds and I had the wave pool drained. I wasn't comfortable having that weight of water over my head, especially when it wasn't being used.

I've gotten up to go several times and each time one or the other has stopped me.

"You can keep us on track. We're so focused on stopping Thorsen's plan we've got tunnel vision," Seb says. "Let's run it again."

"For a dead man, he's certainly giving you the run around."

"Let's go with facts we can verify. Speculation is getting us nowhere."

"Back to the beginning then." Bernie digs through a plethora of files.

"You said he's Norwegian. Did he come over here as a bairn?" I ask.

"No," Bernie says, flipping pages. "He applied to come here in May of 1999. Paperwork was processed fairly quick, application approved early 2000. He arrived in the U.K. in May of that year." He shuffles more paper. "He didn't come to London straighta-way."

"Let me see." Seb holds out a hand. Bernie gives him a sheaf of papers including one that shows a photocopied passport. "He came across the channel from France, commuter special, landed at Shoreham airport on the South Coast. So there's a gap between him arriving in this country and starting work as a 'night security guard' at the Revenue building of..." Seb counts on his fingers, "...three and a half months."

"What did he do before he moved ta this country," I ask, "security work?"

"No idea," Bernie says, shaking the folder as if it might make the missing info fall out.

"Something else to ask Pond," Seb mutters. "Why do I feel like I'm doing this with one hand tied behind my back."

There's a rustle and Bernie hands out plastic sheathed papers. "The stuff our documents people salvaged from the Coltrane/Thorsen gaff."

It's a pretty sorry collection. Thorsen used an ink pen to write on most of the papers. What didn't burn got smudged beyond reading by dirty washing up water.

"This one's typed," Seb says. "He applied for another job and got turned down."

"Where?" Bernie asks, holding out his hand excitedly. "Oh, of course that bit would be burnt to cinders. Know any Latin?" he says to me.

"Amo, amas, amat, amamus, amatis, amant."

"How about 'in dock is pri vata', lo key?"

He hands me the paper. Latin, odd symbols, but I can't shake the idea that I have seen those words before somewhere and recently. That symbol, seal; I'll let my brain chew on it.

"What I don't understand is how the security services fit into Thorsen's plans." Seb rubs his eyes. "Coltrane told me he was expecting us. In fact he said he'd been expecting us sooner. Every piece of the plan we uncover just leads us to another dead end."

"You're not going to like this Sebastian," Bernie says. Seb and I both look at him because I've never heard him use Seb's full name before. "Instead of doing something, we should be doing the opposite."

"Just let the bomb blow up? How is that helping anybody?"

"I said you wouldn't like it lad, but look at the facts. Fact: stolen train, which we found. And if we hadn't, that witness popped up who saw Coltrane and Thorsen stash the train but didn't see Thorsen's demise. Fact: there was a hole cut in the floor of the rear carriage and we found traces of C4 explosive which matched the empty wrapper found in Thorsen's room. And that's it. We've run out of facts."

Seb is shaking his head.

Bernie continues, "I'm worried that something we do; something *you* do, is going to set the rest of his plan in motion."

"No, there's a bomb. There has to be. We know Thorsen bought five blocks of C4. Fact!" I've seen Seb angry, never this angry though. I get up to stop him from walking out but Bernie puts a hand on my arm.

"Let him walk it off, Mary."

"Bernie, he promised to deal with this, staked his career on it. If he does nothing, even if there is no bomb, Pond will still clear parliament and blame him. If he does something, he could inadvertently help a dead mad bomber, and he'll get the blame. Either way he's screwed six ways from Sunday."

Bernie points to the singed papers. "This is Thorsen's *only* mistake. He couldn't have predicted that Worthington's washing would be out on the day he'd told Coltrane to burn his papers. We shouldn't have these; they should be ashes."

We worry away at the notes and still turn up nothing. I give Bernie the key to da's place because he's put away a fair amount of alcohol during the evening and I'm worried he might fall downstairs and break his neck.

I stay up on the roof. The chair is comfortable and I can almost see the stars. I'm also drowsy from the alcohol, and the throw I brought up here with me is easy to snuggle into. The thought that circles the drain as I'm falling asleep, and keeps bugging me, is *why did Coltrane choose that day to burn the documents. If Thorsen left him notes, Seb hasn't said. Maybe it was as simple as a wall calendar with 'burn documents' scrawled on it.*

November 4th 3:00 a.m.

I wave a hand across my face. Something small and cold just hit my cheek, and another and another. I'm stiff as a board. My neck aches. And my head, now I'm awake, begins throbbing in sympathy. The rain, now started, goes from spitting to full on downpour, causing me to jerk upright. The files have gone. I drag myself and the throw downstairs, getting a proper drenching before I can get into the flat. The cold shower causes a sudden hiccup in my brain, Bernie's words from earlier: *'indock is, privata, lo key'.*

My brain was chewing on the symbol and the Latin words in the background, and it spits out that Bernie said that phrase phonetically because he doesn't know any Latin.

"Mary?" Seb's voice interrupts my thoughts. It's coming from the bedroom. He appears, still wearing the clothes he'd stormed out of here in. "Oh my god, I thought you'd gone back to Wandsworth," then, "You're soaked."

He grabs a towel from the bathroom and wraps it around my shoulders. "I'm going to do everything I

can to stop Thorsen's plan," he says, his voiced muffled. "But I can't see how."

"C'mon hen, you need some sleep, and so do I." I
guide him back to the bedroom. We sit on the edge
of the bed and I wrap my arms around him. "I'm nae
goin' anywhere." Then it occurs to me, where did *he*
go?

"I went to see Pond, demanded a look at Thorsen's Norwegian Citizen records. I had to give up
Worthington's position at the Inland Revenue, but
that was a dead end so no harm done.

"We've got until 11:00. That's when he's going to
give the evacuation order. Pond may think I'm done
but I've recruited myself a little inside help."

"Who?"

"Best you don't know. I do have a scrappy theory,
not that it helps us much."

"Tell me."

"Thorsen got a business degree. He went to work
for some pretty questionable people, which is another dead end. However, his family didn't have the
means to pay for the degree courses, so he financed
his tuition by working at ESAC."

"ESAC?"

"Yeah I had to look it up. Think NY school of the performing arts for Circus performers."

"So he can wrangle a herd of elephants? We'd notice those going up Whitehall."

"All the classes he taught or assisted in were in mentalism."

"As in Derren Brown mentalism, as in hypnotizing people?"

I feel him nod in the dark.

"I'd been racking my brains about why Coltrane decided to burn everything on the day we pulled him in for questioning. There were no paper instructions from Thorsen telling him to do that. And he was expecting us to show up days before we actually did."

"You think he somehow programmed Coltrane to burn those papers?"

"I do."

"How?"

"I dunno. It could be something as simple as 'if we get to November 3rd and you're still in the house, meaning not arrested for questioning, then go out and burn the contents of the incinerator' and hey presto!"

"What did you say?"

"Hey Presto or Abracadabra!" he puts a flourish into his voice.

"That's it!" I push myself off the mattress, nearly face planting as the sheet snags my toe. "Shite, sorry." I canter over to my desk, overflowing with papers as usual and start to dig through them, Seb at my heels.

"What got into you?" Seb asks.

"This," I wave the letter head I was looking for. "Indocilis Privata Loqui is the motto of the Magic Circle. Thorsen tried and failed to join the Magic Circle."

"That only proves that he kept up with his magical studies. Wait a minute." The light that has dimmed behind Seb's eyes recently sparks back up, "I've been looking at this all wrong! The people Thorsen used, Coltrane, Lavinia Worthington, the witness, what if he programmed them all?"

"To do what?" I ask. "And who is 'the witness'."

"He's underage. His identity is protected. But don't worry, he's no one you'd know.

"Coltrane and the kid are secure. Lavinia Worthington, to use the chess analogy, is 'still in play'. I'll call the bloke on surveillance and have him follow her, see where she goes."

"Let's go back to bed, we can't do anything until the morning."

"Yeah we can."

"Easy tiger."

"No not *that*.

"You didn't hop a flight to Switzerland so what did Garrett's Doctor have to say for himself."

"He says the complete opposite of what da did."

"Know what the hardest part of my job is? Taking small pieces and turning them into the big picture. Tell me everything the doctor said. Just imagine you're telling me a story; what you said, what he said, how he sounded, what you did."

So I lay there in the dark with Seb's face inches from mine and take both our minds off the fact that the sky is imperceptibly lightening. When I've finished, he goes quiet. I wish he was sleeping, not thinking, but I know better.

"He did let one thing slip," Seb says, his voice thoughtful. "And maybe he did it deliberately. Sounds like he's one of those types that has to prove to the whole room how clever he is."

"What?"

"I think you need to track down Dr. Weiss,"

"Why?"

"Because I think Dr. Weiss may have used another batch of stem cells to augment the ones he extracted from your father to grow new brain cells. Maybe he wanted faster results, maybe the samples got mixed up somehow. I don't pretend to know what motivated him to do that, *if* he did that."

"Da said they were using him as a test case. That would mean there are notes, right?"

"Mary, if you're thinking of going to the clinic to get hold of your dad's case notes, No! A thousand times no! Swiss law is horrendously strict and no one escapes it. I don't want to have to visit you in a Swiss prison. Besides, I have some nerds who can obtain those records for you."

CHAPTER 19

When I woke up just now, Seb was gone. A note on the pillow.

Mary,

I'm going to Parliament, it's where I should be. If I don't get blown to bits, can I interest you in dinner tonight with an unemployed spy.

S

X

If I don't get blown to bits. I can't help thinking that just by saying those words it becomes one of several possible outcomes.

Jo and I are pretty much the only top tier management in the building again. At 10:30 I go out to her,

"I'm going out, Jo. Be back in an hour, it'll all be over by then one way or the other."

"What will be over?" It seems I said that last bit aloud.

"Forget I said it. Early lunch?"

"I'm coming with you," she says, reaching for her coat.

"No! Jo, please trust me. Something might happen today and if it does it'll be bad and I don't want you to get hurt." She subsides and under her breath as I went out I think she said, 'I don't want you getting hurt either'.

Big Ben's striking the quarter hour when I reach Parliament.

"Bonnngggggggggg."

Pond has been totally unoriginal. There are orange warning signs saying 'danger gas leak' and the other side of the road is taped off. People are being herded into Westminster Tube Station, and the roads are closed. The tube exit at Parliament Street is open so I worm myself out onto the street, take out my phone, and call Seb.

"I'm in front of Worthington's building," he says.

"I see you." I hang up and walk down to him. He's leaning against the wall of the customs building. The police guard can't see him because a red phone box is in the way.

"Pond has had Parliament searched from top to bottom," he says, sounding resigned. "Worthington went into work as usual. She's still in there. Higgins is involved in the evacuation but he got me this." He holds up a walkie-talkie. "Pond has taken charge of the operation. He's in there now, putting the fear of god into the civil servants and ministers. They're about to come out and we'll have a front row seat."

"We will?"

"Aye, I mean yes. Higgins clued me into the evacuation plans, once Pond got the Speaker to crack them open. There are several places they can safely stick the MPs. The nearest is right here in the customs building. They'll be walking out in a minute, across the closed off junction and into the front entrance, two by two."

The radio squawks in his hand. "On the move."

"Copy."

"Worthington's in there." I say.

"She's just one woman, and they didn't find any bombs in her handbag. I made sure she was searched, thoroughly." He looks across at the entrance to Parliament. "They should be on the move by now. I wonder what's holding them up."

"Seb?" the voice comes from the radio in his hand.

"Higgins?"

"Mate, we've got a 999 call from the customs building. A women identified as Poppy Cholmond-ley, calling to say she's been assaulted by her boss."

"Copy."

"Mate, hurry, they're halfway there."

"I don't have eyes on."

"Not on street level."

"Dammit!"

Seb, still carrying the radio is running towards the entrance to the customs building. I run after him.

"999 rapid response!" he yells, powering past the police guard who is twice his size but not as fast.

In for a penny I think. "I'm with him," I yell, ducking under the large yellow arm and barreling through the metal detector after Seb. The thing wails like a startled banshee.

Seb stabs the lift call button. It's on this floor so it opens and we both run inside and hit the close door button. The lift hurtles towards the basement.

"Higgins?"

"Copy."

"How far out are you?"

"We're going through Westminster Tube station. I'd say five minutes."

"Stall them."

"I'll try."

The lift doors open to reveal a tear stained Poppy. Her eyes go wide in recognition at both of us.

"Where did she go?" Seb demands.

"The tombs." Poppy sputters.

"Follow us," Seb says, and sprints away, me hard on his heels, Poppy hobbling along behind.

"The one day I choose to wear heels," she pants.

"Open it," Seb orders. "Then get behind me, both of you. She may be armed."

Poppy, hands shaking, keys in the unlock code. Seb charges in, a thud, and when Poppy and I look inside from either side of the door, Seb has Lavinia pinned down on the floor. The security guards arrive and Seb points at the wall. Lavinia Worthington has opened the middle part of the tombs.

The reason we couldn't see a door on Seb's last visit is because the whole wall slides up like one of those awful projector screens we use for PowerPoint presentations. Behind that is a door. Dead centre and attached to it is half the missing block of C4, and a timer with eight minutes left to run.

"Higgins?"

"This is Pond, what the hell Miller?"

"There's an explosive device on our side of the door you are approaching. It has seven minutes left to run."

"Can you defuse it?"

"There's a mercury switch and god knows how many other anti-tamper devices. Go back. I'll deal with this from our end."

"Understood."

Lavinia, still lying on the floor, makes a grab at Seb's ankle. He sidesteps her and one of the security guards drags her away. We hear the clink of handcuffs over the metronome beep of the bomb.

"Poppy," Seb says, "you said this place could withstand a nuclear blast?"

She gives a small nod.

Five minutes remaining.

"All of you start closing these shelves, middle first!" Seb and I turn the wheels. Poppy and the other security guard go to the next ones and we alternate until we have twenty out of twenty four closed down.

"That's it. We're out of time. Move out!" Seb bundles everyone out into Worthington's office. He slams the door shut, locks it, and we move back,

"Keep going!" he yells bringing up the rear.

"That should be far eno." We suddenly find ourselves on the floor. A dull 'boom!' rampages along the corridor. I clamp my hands over my ears to stop the pressure on my eardrums. My bones feel like they went through a blender.

Around me the group are slowly staggering to their feet. The door to the tombs has a massive bow in it, like a giant tried to punch his way out. We can't get the door open, and the explosion didn't tear it from its hinges either.

"How did you know?" There's so much ringing in my ears I have to shout to be heard over it. One of my shoes came off in the melee and I have to slip the other one off so that I don't break my ankle hunting for it.

"I didn't. I guessed, I hoped," Seb yells back over his own personal carillon. We're all grinning and back slapping, not dying has that effect. The security men have forgotten that they were chasing us down here; that they thought we were a threat.

Seb is now very much in charge.

"You should evacuate this building just to be on the safe side," he says, well, shouts. One of the security team pulls the fire alarm. I scoop up my errant shoe; there's a big scratch across the front. In my tootsies, I follow the emergency evacuation route up the stairs to street level. A flood of civil servants is not something you see every day. The older ones seem half asleep, the younger ones form groups, islands, which the older ones flow around. We're close to the exit. I step out of the traffic flow and slip into my shoes.

"I'm going to check on the other end of the tunnel," Seb yells, drawing unintended attention.

"Right, be careful, hen," I try and modulate my voice so that I'm nae bawling back at him.

He plants a soft kiss on my cheek, then cuts into the line by flashing his ID. Coming out into the street makes my heart lift because a few moments ago I had visions of the roof coming down on us, courtesy of bloody Thorsen.

We beat ya, you numpty, I think. Trooping down the stairs, in my head I'm high kicking down them like Angela Rippon in that Morecombe and Wise Christmas Special da loves so much.

"Oooooooohh!"

Around me the plod increases to a scuttle. I flip a quick look over my shoulder and see the reason. Poppy, in full dive. The scene shifts into slow motion as she cartwheels down the steps, knocking civil servants down left and right like bowling pins in a winning strike. I try and dodge out of the way and I'm almost clear when her flailing foot connects with the back of my knee sending me flying off to the side. Now I'm off balance, simultaneously attempting not to fall while helplessly watching Poppy mow down more people. She finishes with a face plant 'splat!' onto the pavement that makes me wince, almost counteracting the flare of pain that explodes in my leg and blossoms into blissful unconsciousness.

CHAPTER 20

If they'd asked me, which they didn't, I'd say I remember flashes. The sirens from a fleet of ambulances, being lifted onto a stretcher, mumbling for water because my throat was parched, feeling the magnetic pull of blackness, alternating between fighting it and welcoming the release from the screaming nerves in my leg and higher. When I wake up proper, I don't open my eyes, I listen; medical beeps and clicks, and smell; the reek of cloying disinfectant. Even though I can't see it, I can sense a needle in my arm. I focus on my leg and can't feel *anything*. Panicked, I flick my eyes open, which is actually a slow blink because they were gummed shut. My leg is still there. My whole body shudders when I think about why they could be giving me morphine. I flash back to what happened to my half-brother in a hospital bed just like this. Then angrily tell ma self to get a grip. The door to my room is open, a private room. I could even be in the same private wing as Fergus and Seb were last year. I let my thoughts drift, trying to piece together what happened.

Then, as if I've conjured him, I think I hear Seb's voice.

"I got here as soon as I could. What the hell happened?"

"That must've been one humdinger of a debrief," says Higgins.

"I had to explain my part in all of this, and so far, for once Pond's the one in hot water. Can I see her?"

"You'd have to ask her Doctor, mate." I've been sitting out here keeping an eye cos I thought you'd want me to. She's still out cold."

"What happened?"

"More like who happened. Worthington's assistant, Poppy. Freak accident. Her heel broke at the top of the stairs and she fell, injured more than a dozen people on her plummet down the steps. I saw the whole thing. But I couldn't get to them in time, too far away. One of the old timers had a heart attack. Poppy's going to be okay but her face is going to need a lot of work."

"Sod Poppy!" Hearing Seb curse Poppy makes the peeping sound of my heart rate go up just enough that they notice.

"Excuse me! Doctor!"

"Stay out here please. You can't both be family."

"I'm her boyfriend, and he..."

"Can stay outside, MI6 ID or no."

I squeeze ma eyes shut, knowing that if Seb and the Doctor talk 'man to man' I'll find out exactly what is wrong with my bally leg. Seb knows me well enough to not sugar coat it, but for some ridiculous reason men who've never met me think I'm some delicate flower that will scorch under their full attention. Case in point.

"We should talk in my office, Mr...?"

"...Miller. And here is fine. Did she break her leg in the fall?"

"She overextended her hip joint. Imagine twisting a flannel to wring water out of it. She did that both ways and when she fell she landed on the bone and fractured it. She twisted her knee as well, but that will heal."

"She broke her hip? She's thirty, not sixty!"

I broke my hip, what the...?

"Fractured, not broke," the Doctor corrects. "Freak accident. It could happen to anyone in the right set of circumstances. The twisting, the fall, gravity, they all added up."

Okay now I know. I don't flutter my eyelids. I stare straight at where I can hear them. "I broke my hip?" I sound awful, parched.

"Fractured," the Doctor corrects, as I get my eyes open again.

"Can you glue me back together?" I ask, taking the plastic cup of water Seb has poured for me. Struggling to sit up, I feel his hand on my back, raising me gently until my lips and the water cup connect, I suck it down and, one handed. he fills it again.

"Ms. Maccallan, you aren't a dropped vase. We can't just repair you with super glue." I fix him with my best boardroom stare. "There are options though." To Seb, "She needs rest."

"I promise I won't tire her out." Seb closes the door and pulls up a chair.

"How much trouble is Pond in?" I croak.

"Schadenfreude, Mary?"

"Aye, a terrible case of it, but I'll live. Spill it."

"Pond may have to resign his post at MI6."

Seb explains that the MP's heard our exchanges on the radio and, to a man (and woman), they pointed out that Pond would have led them into the path of the explosion if Seb hadn't warned Higgins.

"You get yer job back and Pond gets the boot. That's a result."

"Not really."

"I'm nae following, hen."

"I might lose my job for good if Pond 'gets the boot', as you so generously put it."

"I told you, with your experience..." I can feel the tiredness seeping into my bones, or maybe that's the morphine. "...You could waltz into a head of security position wi' no messin'."

"Soon, maybe."

"You're not going to go back to nocturnal activities again are ye?"

"No, I was going to book a plane ticket to Dubai, and I was hoping you'd come with me. But now..."

"I'm going to be out of commission for a few weeks, hen. Go to Dubai. Find your sister. I'll be here when you come back."

He kisses me softly on the cheek, "I'll stay till you fall asleep."

One week later:

Since I came around from the operation, my room has been a revolving door of visitors. Jo was first, accompanied by Philly. They brought papers with headlines of an emergency evacuation drill gone wrong, and because Jo knows I hate grapes, she smuggled me a Cadbury's chocolate orange. Daz has gone back to Mumbai for his brother's funeral. He sent me a giant bunch of flowers and a promise to visit as soon as he gets back.

Now I have a dilemma. Physically da is fine; mentally we still don't know. The timing of this couldn't be worse. I was discussing it with Philly and Jo just yesterday and Jo had an idea, which is to call a special board meeting. I'm banking on their technophobia to have this work. Jo sent letters, which makes it official, and emails asking the MAC to RSVP and attend a meeting in my hospital room this afternoon at 3:00.

3:15:

"I call this meeting to order." I bang the gavel that Jo brought along on the metal rail of my bed. It gives off a hollow 'bong'.

Three of the MAC have shown up, not enough to form a quorum against me. Also attending: Jo, who is taking notes and brought Lee's video camera to memorialize the event, and Philly who is integral to my plans, although she doesn't know it yet.

After all the arcane bollocks of introduction has been dispensed with, I put forward my proposal.

"As all of you know, I will be in recovery for a least another month, maybe longer depending on what the surgeon has to say. Here is what I propose. We need someone running the day to day, and that isn't someone on painkillers who keeps dozing off in the middle of a sentence."

Behind the MAC, who are clustered next to my bed like the three freaking wise men, sans gifts, I catch Jo biting her lip before any mirth can form. I could be describing the MAC and it goes totally over their heads. Good job she's behind the camera.

"So my thought is that the best person to be doing this is Ms. Forrester." Philly's surprised 'O' face is recorded for posterity. "Let me walk you through my reasoning for this," I say, trying to get in quick before Philly starts to protest. "Ms. Forrester is organized, competent, can think on her feet in a crisis, has an equally competent deputy that could do her job in her absence and it would only be for three months." Here I look straight at Philly, pleading. If she baulks and refuses to take the reins, my plan is unworkable. "I would still be involved, but as deputy CEO. This plan would facilitate my recovery and also keep Garrett from being saddled with CEO duties when he, too, needs to be recovering and strengthening his mental faculties."

One of the MAC turns to Philly. Crunch time.

"Mizzz Forrester, this is highly unusual. But as the current CEO points out, it would only be for three months. Do you feel able to take on the position?"

All eyes turn to Philly. After a dog's age, which is probably only a few minutes, she nods.

"I would be willing to take this on. I won't lie, I'm surprised, and a little shocked to be nominated. However, my deputy, Selima can keep my seat warm and..." she colours, "...I would be honoured to accept."

"Now," says another MAC member, I really should get them name tags so that I can tell them apart. "My colleagues and I will adjourn to the corridor and consider our votes."

That wasn't in the plan and I almost tell them that we should vote here and now.

I check my watch. "I have some pills coming at 3:30. Let's try and have a resolution before the meeting becomes unsecured." My voice almost cracks. I reach for the water pitcher, pour myself a slug, and sip it. If I gulp it down, I run the risk of choking on it.

The time crawls by. Philly can't fully express herself, although I can see that she's going to give me hell when the camera is turned off.

The MAC who went out into the corridor file back in.

"Are we ready to vote?" I ask. They nod.

"Show of hands. Who approves Ms. Forrester as temporary CEO?"

Two hands go up; mine and the nearest MAC.

"Against?"

The other two fossils put their hands up. Aaaaand we're deadlocked!

"Hmm," Jo raises her hand. "According to the articles, when there's a tie, the CEO gets the casting vote."

"She's already voted!"

"I'm only quoting the articles. And I wasn't talking about Mary, I was talking about Garrett Maccallan." Jo, I could hug you.

"To keep it impartial, which I'm sure your fellow board members would demand, I can Skype Mr. Maccallan, give him the proposal, describe the deadlock, and he casts the deciding vote."

After a bit of hemming and hawing, the MAC agrees. Jo, witnessed by those attending this meeting and on camera calls Garrett. I have visions of him not answering, being in the middle of sponge bath, or on the loo.

"Hello, Jo? Is something the matter? Where's ma daughter?"

Jo smoothly précis the meeting so far, assuring him that I'm fine and present but mute, and that the meeting is being recorded to keep everything above board.

"We have a tie on a proposal. Your casting vote would be appreciated."

The old Garrett's pre dodgy brain connections would've processed the information in no time flat and given us an answer. I wonder how long it will take this time. He's gone silent. I know he hired Philly after extensive interviews, and like Alex he emphasized that she has integrity in spades. This move is genius on Jo's part because Garrett simply has to judge if Philly can do the job. But it could backfire if he thinks Philly is being used by one of the board to unseat me. Seriously, this lot would give Machiavelli the screamin' ab dabs. Right on cue the blasted nurse comes in and orders the others to clear the room. They leave, taking da and the camera with them. The pain killers that replaced the morphine, something called Percocet, mess with my head as well as ma pain, leaving me a little loopy. I've done my best to stay awake, but I could feel the things wearing off during the meeting. My fault for thinking we could get this done in half an hour. I don't want to fall asleep, but I do.

CHAPTER 21

No one is at my bedside when I wake up. I don't see the note straight away; it's tucked between the plastic cup and the water jug.

MARY

GARRETT VOTED YES

HE WANTS TO TALK TO YOU

Using the control button to raise my back rest up, I wrestle the lap top onto my stomach and call him.

As usual he looks clear eyed. It's been that way since he had the first infusion nearly six months ago.

"Lassie," he leans into the screen, "you look tired."

"Thanks da. You make a girl feel so special. I'm doped up to ma eyeballs and I just woke up. Jo told me the results. If you want to read me the riot act I might fall asleep in the middle of it. Are you willing to take the risk?"

"I have some news," he says, riding roughshod over any complaints I might have. He clearly doesn't know I was for the proposal and that's no surprise. Philly and I have kept our office relationship on the level of 'possible frenemy' because I didn't want her to get caught in the MACs disapproval of me.

"Go ahead."

"Orlov's been removed."

"That is good news."

"The new specialist has ordered another series of scans. I'll let you know as soon as he gives me the results."

"Do me a favour. Don't call me at 2 in the morning."

"That only happened once and it was a misdial." This makes me wonder who he meant to dial that early in the morning.

"Maybe I should come out there and get them to grow me a new hip bone instead of this ceramic one."

"Nonsense, lassie! That thing will outlast ye. And best of all, you won't set off the metal detectors at the airport like your Uncle Hamish used to with his tin..., what's the matter?"

"Oh, nothing. Just tired."

"Night lassie."

"Night da."

His face fades from the screen. I try and get some rest but the thought that I don't have, and to ma ken have never had, an Uncle Hamish, spins around keeping me awake. In the end, I hit the call button and request a couple of sleeping pills from the duty nurse. And I'm rewarded with a cup of chamomile tea because sleeping pills and Perc don't mix well.

The next day (Saturday):

I slept like a log last night. But the worry popped up again two seconds after I woke up this morning, along with the draining feeling that tells me the painkillers are all but worn off. When the nurse came in with my scrambled egg on toast and Perc, I ask for my laptop. She hands it over on the way out, along with an admonition to 'take your pills'. Google has a lot of things to say about Percocet, including drug interactions and risk of addiction.

When my surgeon, Dr. Gupta does his rounds, I ask him for something other than Perc.

"Is it not working?" Gupta asks.

"It's working, but when it stops working, it's like falling off a cliff. It was all I could do not to down those pills before you came in."

"You are a most unusual patient," Gupta observes. "I rarely have my decisions queried." He smiles with his perfect teeth and his caramel skin. I wonder if, around here, they only employ surgeons who conform to the golden ratio of facial perfection. His brown eyes hold an amused hint of rebuke. He sits down on the edge of the bed.

"Can you move?" he asks.

"Not unless you want me screaming in your ear, doc." He hands me the pills and the water.

"On a scale of 1-10 how bad is the pain right this minute?"

"Eleven plus."

"Take the pills and then we'll talk." I obediently pop them into my mouth and wash them down.

"I've felt your pain, literally. Had a skiing accident on holiday many years ago and ended up with a Swiss doctor resetting my smashed up shoulder. I was a junior doctor then, and he told me that this kind of pain was like a wild animal. The pills kept it leashed. Once they wore off, it took the pain a little while to work out that it was free to bite at my nerve endings again."

As he's speaking, liquid sunshine is flowing through ma veins. Pain? What pain? What was I saying? With a mighty effort I pull my focus back to Gupta. "I feel like I'm going doolally tap. I'd rather be in full possession of ma faculties, doc. Pain or no."

"Ms. Maccallen, I don't advise going cold turkey."

"On that doc we agree, but I've been researching, and Percocet scares the hell out of me. I want to wean myself off them."

"Doing my job for me." Again the rebuke is gentle, but it's there. "There are other means of pain relief. Some of them are regarded as too 'woo woo' by several of my less enlightened colleagues. Some of them aren't even legal."

"I'd like to think I'm open minded. Hit me with the 'woo woo' doc."

"I'll schedule you some 'alternative therapy' for later today," he says with a wink. "Now float for a bit."

The 'therapy' arrives after lunch. A nurse, with the same last name as my surgeon, gauges my pain on the 1-10 scale. When we get to a seven, she teaches me something she calls 'breath work'. Each time a wave of pain builds, rather than resisting it, she tells me to welcome it with open arms and do the breathing techniques she shows me. (4x4x4 and fire breathing, which involves panting like an excited puppy).

"Keep practicing them. It will feel strange to start with, and you won't 'get it' straight away." She goes on to fill in a bit of background, how we don't breathe deep enough. "Many types of yoga incorporate these kinds of breath work; the positions and the breath together. If you feel you are doing it wrong, stop and rehearse what we did and then go again."

"It can't hurt, I s'pose."

She stays with me for an hour, during which my pain spikes at an eight. She brings in ma pills and makes sure I've swallowed them.

"I'll come back tomorrow. Keep practicing. In fact practice every hour. We'll work towards having you take the Percocet at bed time, and lowering the doses you take during the day."

"Y'know if it ever gets out that I'm doing this I'll be a bloody laughing stock," I say to her on the second day, after doing the more advanced fire breathing technique through my nose. I sound like a caffeinated truffle pig.

"It's working right?" She looks down her nose at me.

"Well, yeah. Well, I think so,"

"How's your pain level."

"Six to a seven. Better."

"Here's a little bit of advice. If you don't make a big thing of it. If you just practice these techniques in your office, or in the back of a taxi, or in bed, no one else will know that you're even doing them. I have taught my husband to meditate instead of sleep when he's on call at work. No one else knows he does it, and the gossip is that he's taking something to keep himself so mentally alert."

"Wow."

Monday:

"How are you this morning?" Gupta asks me the question after breakfast, which I noticed didn't come with the usual side order of pills.

"I slept right through." I attempt to stretch and yawn like a normal person, and wince as the pain nips me. We go over the pain scale again, and I do more breathing exercises, until I'm hovering at a 'six'.

"If you continue to progress like this we'll have you in the hands of our physiotherapist (he says it with a hard 't' which makes it sound like physioterrorist) in no time. And painkillers or not, the sooner we get you up on crutches, the less muscle we have to build back up. Don't be a martyr though."

10:00 a.m.:

I just heard from Jo that Philly is installed in ma office and Jo is showing her the ropes. And so far she is showing no signs of wanting to jump out of my office window. As I replace the receiver onto its cradle, Bernie saunters in. He's on the list of approved visitors; they have one of those now. All staff have to have security checks carried out on them twice a year because of what happened to my half-brother whilst in their care. I made sure that Pond is *not* on the approved list.

"I bring grapes and news." Seeing my face, he says, "kidding. I bring an apple turnover from that deli you like. I did bring an espresso too, but the nurs-zi on the desk relieved me of it."

"The thought is appreciated, hen. They have enough reasons for my blood pressure to go sky high without adding pure caffeine to the mix."

"Where's the morning cocktail of meds?" He gestures to the bedside cabinet.

"Who says I haven't already taken them?"

"Me. No empty paper thimble, your water jug is full, and the drinking cup is dry."

"Aren't we observant this morning, hen?"

"Old habits," Bernie says. "Frankly, the younger generation are getting soft; too reliant on painkillers. When I was in my prime I used pain to keep my mind sharp, and if you like I can teach you a couple of pain management techniques."

"Nae, hen, I've got ma own onsite yogini."

As he mentioned being in his prime, I can't help throwing out the question.

"You were a real life Liam Neeson for MI6, weren't you?"

"You've been reading too many spy stories, Mary." He winks. "We're accountable now. Having assassins on Queenie's payroll would lead to questions in Whitehall, and an enquiry by the Daily Mail. I only shoot clays."

And when you weren't accountable?

Bernie drags a chair over to the bed and sinks into it.

"I had a call from Seb this morning. He's at Dubai airport, heading for Europe. He tried calling you but you didn't pick up."

"Did he say anything more about Domino?"

"Only that the bird has flown."

"Oh Seb," I murmur. I can feel a gnawing from my hip. *Breathe.*

"Poor sod. What with all the fall-out from..."

"Fall out. What fall out?"

Bernie, gets to his feet. "Is that the time. I've got things to do. I'll visit again soon."

"Bernie!"

The door closes behind him. I'd go after him if I was able.

"Buggerbuggerbugger!!"

I sink back onto the pillows, vowing to myself that sooner rather than later, I'm going to walk out of here.

Right now all I can do is commiserate by snaffling the apple turnover, which is probably worse for me than the coffee would've been. Then it occurs to me that Seb might've left a voice mail. My phone was on the side next to the water jug last night. Now there's an empty space. I huff annoyance through my nose. One of the nurses, I've yet to work out which one because the sneaky wee cow does it at night whilst I'm asleep, keeps moving my phone into the drawer of the bedside unit. I've almost fallen out of the bed trying to reach it several times. I reach for the call button. *Breathe, get the pain down to a seven or a six.*

The door swings open and, caught in the act of eating contraband, I swipe any crumbs from my lips and cover the remaining corner of the turnover with my other hand. It's not a nurse, it's Higgins, whom I haven't seen since, well heard, since November 4th.

One of the cadre of nurses that work here appears at his shoulder, eases her way past him, picks up my chart from the foot of the bed, peruses it, places the pills in their paper sheath on the table, asks if I need the loo, pours a slug of water, and with a pointed look at the pills I haven't yet reached for, she leaves.

"You want to take those?" Higgins asks.

"Not yet." In case he thinks I'm on some kind of masochist kick I add, "I'm trying to wean myself off 'em." I wince and once again breathe deeper into my diaphragm than I knew I could.

"They should be giving you morphine."

"They were. I did nae want my senses scrambled by *anything*."

Breathe.

Higgins takes the chair vacated by Bernie.

"I've been meaning to visit but it's been hell on wheels at work. I promised Seb I'd look in on you."

"New suit?" Higgins has entered the world of bespoke tailoring. When he sits down the suit hugs, instead of bulging at the lapels like his old ones did.

"New everything, I got promoted. I'm currently second in command to the Chief whilst she gets her sea legs under her, hopefully longer."

"M's a woman now?"

"Between you and me, I think she's part tiger. I watched her rip the P.M to shreds a couple of days ago."

"I know people, me included, who'd pay money to see that." I skootch around trying to find a find a more comfortable position. Opening the door to more pain and another round of deep breathing.

"Are you okay?" Higgins asks. I nod. Unlike Bernie, Higgins is probably happier popping pills, although I may be doing him a massive disservice thinking that.

"Aye. Could you open that drawer and hand me ma phone?"

Higgins tries to hide the worried look, gives up, and retrieves my phone. He grins as I take it and expose the remains of the pastry.

"Any other stuff you need smuggling in?"

"I'd kill for some salted dark chocolate." The phone shows several flashing icons including the tape loop, indicating I do have a voicemail.

An awkward silence descends. I can almost hear him asking *'so how are they treating you?'* and before he can I jump in.

"Is the Thorsen thing all wrapped up?"

We get all the papers in here and there has been radio silence about the real events of November 4th. I'm still amazed at the way they can take some of the facts and wrap them into a completely different scenario.

"You understand there's only so much I can tell you." I nod, my mouth now full of apple turnover. "We followed the money and it took a while to trace it back to a source.

"Thorsen's plans were financed by a foreign power. We know which one, but it's need-to-know, and you don't. We can prove they bought him the C4. We suspect the house in Wimbledon was also leased with their help. It was part of a blatant attempt to destabilize her majesty's government. We have to stay on our toes," he says. "God knows what they might try next. I wish we still had Seb with us. It wasn't his fault he wasn't officially an agent when he let that bomb go off, and I argued that with M but she wasn't having it. Five wanted him. I mean properly wanted him, but of course they waited too long and now he's..."

"He's what?"

"...going private. I'm sure he was going to tell you as soon as he got back from Dubai."

The pain ambushes me. No amount of deep breathing is going to stem this one.

"First Bernie, now you! Stop treating me with kid gloves. I'm no gonna break!" I yell, snatching the pills and the water and knocking them back so fast I almost choke. I can feel ma face reddening and ma pulse ticking up.

"There was an enquiry. Seb wasn't officially an agent of MI6 when he breached security at the customs building. His actions in saving the lives of the MPs were taken into consideration. They told him he could resign or face charges of impersonating an officer of the crown, destruction of property and assault."

"Those ungrateful bastards!"

"There are things you don't know. When the bomb went off it vaporized all the records in the tombs, and it also cracked the foundation. All of Customs and Excise have had to relocate to Manchester until they can fix the building, and that will cost the taxpayer millions of pounds. And the security people said that Seb didn't even attempt to defuse the bomb, he just shut the doors and let it go off."

I know that's not true. I wonder if my testimony could've saved Seb's job while damning Pond. Seb must've known he was in trouble before he left for Dubai. I wish he had asked me to help him. Ceramic hip or no I'd have gone to bat for him, but he never asked. I can feel my anger building, not at Seb, at the establishment he cares so much about, which just cast him off like some disposable napkin.

"Higgins? Please leave now, or I can't guarantee your safety."

He takes one look at me and leaves the room.

Seconds later, the vase of flowers that were minding their own business and hurting no one, go hurtling across the room, smashing into the wall. A couple of choking sobs, have the gall to come out of my mouth. I swallow them down. The Percocet spreading like antifreeze, is muddling ma thoughts. I fumble the phone and almost delete the voicemail.

Seb's voice, tinny.

"Mary, I'm coming home. Domino won't talk to me and it feels like I'm wasting my time when I should be there with you. I'll be flying to Switzerland first. I want to check on your dad. I'm about to go through security. Call me back. Or I'll call you when I land in Zurich."

My da?

I call him. "Hey hen."

"Hi Mary."

"Sorry I didn't call you. The bally nurses keep hiding ma phone."

"I'll be back home in a day or so. There's a couple of anomalies I want to check out."

"With da in Switzerland?"

"It's probably nothing."

"And if it turns into 'something'?"

"It won't."

'Cos if it did turn into 'something', I'd want to know, hen. Keeping me in the dark hurts both of us."

"Er. What's that noise?" A couple of double beeps sound in my ear.

"Email," I say. I want to get back to the anomalies but know full well that he's surrounded by people. He tries changing the subject, and for now I let him, but I'm no done with him yet.

"Something else I need to tell you, Mary. I, I haven't been entirely honest with you. I've been talking with your surgeon every day. I wanted to wait until you could handle what I'm about to tell you without, I dunno, chucking something at the wall." I look guiltily in the direction of the smashed vase and the single carnation pasted to the paintwork.

"I still have a job," he continues, "just not with the old firm."

"Six flyer-ed you?" The pills are hijacking my tongue. I sound sloshed. "Hoots, hen, I'm nae plastered. It's the pills."

"You're forgetting I had the same experience last year," he laughs softly. "And yes, we've officially parted ways. I'm still in the same field, just a little lower down the totem pole than I used to be."

"Still an agent?"

"Sort of." There's rustling and then the voices quieten.

"Mary, I wanted to say something in private. I wanted to say it the day we met, but that would've been weird." Again the double beep. I wave it away like an annoying gnat. "We've been together for a while now and I still feel that I could jinx this by saying it aloud but what the hell. Mary Maccallan, I lo..."

"Hello? Hen?" I shake the phone, which has become a paperweight. The bloody thing's run out of charge. I stab the call button to get a charger, a new battery, anything to get him back on the line. After the longest half an hour of my life the phone has enough charge in it but by then he's in the air.

"The number for," the voice intones Seb's phone number, "is not available. Please leave a message after the tone."

"Seb, it's me. I don't think you've thought this through. You've no badge to wave at those Swiss clinic people. I'm redirecting Charlie, dad's lawyer, you remember him? I'll ask him to fly out and meet you at the clinic. Don't go there without him. Here's his number." I reel off Charlie's number and hope I can intercept him before he leaves Hong Kong. "I love you. Come home soon." is what I start to say, except a flurry of beeps drowns ma voice out. I hang up feeling strangely empty.

The phone rings again.

"Mary?"

"Philly?"

"Special Branch just swooped in," her voice wobbles, "they've arrested Jo!"

TO BE CONCLUDED

About the Author

Paula Longhurst is the author of A Case of Espionage and has been reading thrillers since the age of 10. She works at The King's English Bookstore in Salt Lake City, UT where she'll happily sell you a good twisted mystery or two. When not writing, Paula loves foreign travel with husband Chris, spirited conversation and time spent with friends and family. She is currently hard at work on the next Mary Maccallan novel.

For more information go to Paula Longhurst Writer on Facebook, email her at paulalonghurstwriter@gmail.com or visit her blog englishrosesloverain.blogspot.com

www.ingramcontent.com/pod-product-compliance
Lightning Source LLC
Chambersburg PA
CBHW020948120726
47905CB00008B/2730